Penguin Book 2521
Drunkard's Walk

Frederik Pohl was born on the twenty-sixth
of November, 1919. Although he has devoted
his literary career to writing science fiction,
of the (approximately) fifty books which he has
had published, ten have been miscellaneous
fiction and non-fiction in other fields.
For his general contributions to science fiction,
he was awarded the 'Invisible Little Man'
trophy at the 1964 World Science Fiction
Convention in California. On a higher level, he
has been invited to address scientific and
technical gatherings with the impressive titles
of 'Diebold Research Group Conference'
or 'Drexel Institute Conference on Technical
Information' and has appeared on nearly
200 radio and television programmes in the
United States and Canada.

Since 1961 he has been the editor of *Galaxy*
and *If* and, since 1963, of *Worlds of
Tomorrow*; three science-fiction magazines. He
has also contributed to periodicals ranging from
American Documentation to *Playboy*.

Frederik Pohl is a volunteer fireman and
elected official of the Democratic Party and
lives with his wife and four children in New
Jersey.

Frederik Pohl
Drunkard's Walk
Penguin Books

Penguin Books Ltd, Harmondsworth,
Middlesex, England
Penguin Books Pty Ltd, Ringwood,
Victoria, Australia

First published in the U.S.A. 1960
Published in Great Britain by Victor Gollancz 1961
Published in Penguin Books 1966

Made and printed in Great Britain by
Hunt Barnard & Co. Ltd, Aylesbury

Set in Monotype Baskerville

Chapter One

This man's name is Cornut, born in the year 2166 and now thirty. He is a teacher.

Mathematics is his discipline. Number Theory is his speciality. He instructs the Mnemonics of Number, a study which absorbs all his creative thought. But he also thinks about girls a lot; in a detached, remote sort of way.

He is unmarried. He sleeps alone and that is not so good.

If you wander around his small bedroom (it has lilac walls and a cream ceiling, those are the Math Tower colours), you will hear a whispering and a faint whirring sound. These are not the sounds of Cornut's breath, although he is sleeping peacefully. The whispering is a hardly audible *wheep, wheep* from an electric clock. (It was knocked to the floor once. A gear is slightly off axis; it rubs against a rivet.) The whir is another clock. If you look more carefully you will find that there are more clocks.

There are five clocks in this room, all told. They all have alarms, set to ring at the same moment.

Cornut is a good-looking man, even if he is a little pale. If you are a woman (say, one of the girls in his classes), you would like to get him out in the sun. You would like to fatten him up and make him laugh more. He is not aware that he needs sunshine or fattening, but he is very much aware that he needs something.

He knows something is wrong. He has known this for seven weeks, on the best evidence of all.

The five clocks march briskly towards seven-fifteen, the time at which they are set to go off. Cornut has spent a lot of time arranging it so that they will sound at the same moment. He set the alarm dial on each, checked it by revolving the hands of the clocks themselves to make note of the exact second at which the trigger went off, painfully reset and rechecked. They are now guaranteed to ring, clang or buzz within a quarter-minute of each other.

However, one of them has a bad habit. It is the one that Cornut dropped once. It makes a faint click a few moments before the alarm mechanism itself rings.

It clicks now.

The sound is not very loud, but Cornut stirs. His eyes flicker. They close again, but he is not quite asleep.

After a moment he pushes back the covers and sits up. His eyes are still almost closed.

Suppose you are a picture on his wall – perhaps the portrait of Leibniz, taken from Ficquet's old engraving. Out of the eyes under your great curled wig you see this young man stand up and walk slowly towards his window.

His room is eighteen storeys up.

If a picture on the wall can remember, you remember that this is not the first time. If a picture on the wall can know things, you know that he has tried to leap out of that window before, and he is about to try again.

He is trying to kill himself. He has tried nine times in the past fifty days.

If a picture on a wall can regret, you regret this. It is a terrible waste for this man to keep trying to kill himself, since he does not at all want to die.

Chapter Two

Cornut was uncomfortable in his sleep. He felt drowsily that he had worked himself into an awkward position, and besides, someone was calling his name. He mumbled, grimaced, opened his eyes.

He was looking straight down, nearly two hundred feet.

At once he was fully awake. He teetered dangerously, but someone behind him had caught him by an arm, someone who was shouting at him. Whoever it was, he pulled Cornut roughly back into the room.

At that moment the five alarm clocks burst into sound, like a well-drilled chorus; a beat later the phone by his bed rang; the room lights sprang into life, controlled by their automatic timer; one reading lamp turned and fitted with a new, brighter tube so that it became a spotlight aimed at the pillow where Cornut's head should have been.

'*Are you all right?*'

The question had been repeated several times, Cornut realized. He said furiously, 'Of course I'm all right!' It had been very close; his veins were suddenly full of adrenalin, and as there was nothing else for it to do it charged him with anger . . . . 'I'm sorry. Thanks, Egerd.'

The undergraduate let go. He was nineteen years old, with crew-cut red hair and a face that was normally deeply tanned, now almost white. 'That's all right.' He cautiously backed to the phone, still watching the professor. 'Hello. Yes, he's awake now. Thanks for calling.'

'They were almost too late,' said Cornut. Egerd shrugged.

'I'd better get back, sir. I'll have to – Oh, good morning, Master Carl.'

The house-master was standing in the doorway, a gaggle of undergraduates clustered behind him like young geese, staring in to see what all the commotion was. Master Carl was tall, black-haired, with eyes like star sapphires. He stood holding a wet photographic negative that dripped gently on to the rubber tiles. 'What the devil is going on here?' he demanded.

Cornut opened his mouth to answer, and then realized how utterly impossible it was for him to answer that question. He didn't know! The terrible thing about the last fifty days was just that. He didn't know what, he didn't know why, all he knew was that this was the ninth time he had very nearly taken his own life, 'Answer Master Carl, Egerd,' he said.

The undergraduate jumped. Carl was the central figure in his life; every student's hope of passing, of graduating, of avoiding the military draft or forced labour in the Assigned Camps lay in his house-master's whim. Egerd said, stammering, 'Sir, I – I have been on extra duty for Master Cornut. He asked me to come in each morning five minutes before wake-up time and observe him, because he – That is, that's what he asked me to do. This morning I was a little late.'

Carl said coldly, 'You were late?'

'Yes, sir. I – '

'And you came into the corridor without *shaving?*'

The undergraduate was struck dumb. The cluster of students behind Carl briskly dissolved. Egerd started to speak, but Cornut cut in. He sat down shakily on the edge of his bed. 'Leave the boy alone, will you, Carl? If he had taken time to shave I'd be dead.'

Master Carl rapped out, 'Very well. You may go to your room, Egerd. Cornut, I want to know what this is all about. I intend to get a full explanation. . . .' He paused, as though remembering something. He glanced down at the wet negative in his hand.

'As soon as we've had breakfast,' he said grimly, and stalked majestically back to his own rooms.

Cornut dressed heavily, and began to shave. He had aged a full year every day of the past seven weeks; on that basis, he calculated, he was already pushing eighty and a full decade older than Master Carl himself.

Seven weeks. Nine attempts at suicide.

And no explanation.

He didn't look like a man who had just sleepwalked himself to the narrow edge of suicide. He was young for a professor and built like an athlete, which was according to the facts; he had been captain of the fencing team as an undergraduate, and was its faculty advisor still. His face looked like the face of a husky, healthy youth who for some reason had been cutting himself short on sleep, and that was also according to the facts. His expression was that of a man deeply embarrassed by some incredibly inexcusable act he has just committed. And that fitted the facts too.

Cornut *was* embarrassed. His foolishness would be all over the campus by now; undoubtedly there had been whispers before, but this morning's episode had had many witnesses and the whispers would be quite loud. As the campus was Cornut's whole life, that meant that every living human being whose opinion counted with him at

9

all would soon be aware that he was fecklessly trying to commit suicide – for no reason – and not even succeeding!

He dried his face and got ready to leave his room – which meant facing them, but there was no way out of that. A bundle of letters and memoranda were in the mail hopper by his desk. He paused to look at them: nothing important. He glanced at his notes, which someone had been straightening. Probably Egerd. His scrawled figures on the Wolgren anomalies were neatly stacked on top of the *schema* for this morning's lectures; in the centre of the desk, with a paperweight on top of it, was the red-bordered letter from the President's Office, inviting him to go on the Field Expedition. He reminded himself to ask Carl to get him off that. He had too much to do to waste time on purely social trips. The Wolgren study alone would keep him busy for weeks, and Carl was always pressing him to publish. But that was premature. Three months from now . . . maybe . . . if Computer Section allocated enough time, and if the anomalies didn't disappear in someone's ancient error in simple addition.

And if he was still alive, of course.

'Oh, damn it all, anyhow,' Cornut said suddenly. He tucked the President's letter into his pocket, picked up his cape and walked irritably out into the hall.

The Math Tower dining-room served all thirty-one masters of the department, and most of them were there before him. He walked in with an impassive face, expecting a sudden hush to stop the permanent buzz of conversation in the hall, and getting it. Everyone was looking at him.

'Good morning,' he said cheerfully, nodding all around the room.

One of the few women on the staff waved to him, giggling. 'Good for you, Cornut! Come sit with us, will you? Janet has an idea to help you stop suiciding!'

Cornut smiled and nodded and turned his back on the two women. They slept in the women's wing, twelve storeys below his own dorms, but already the word had spread. Naturally. He stopped at the table where Master Carl sat alone, drinking tea and looking through a sheaf of photographs. 'I'm sorry about this morning, Carl,' he said.

Master Carl looked vaguely up at him. Dealing with his equals, Carl's eyes were not the brittle star-sapphires that had pierced Egerd; they were the mild, blue eyes of a lean Santa Claus, which was much closer to his true nature. 'Oh? Oh. You mean about jumping out of the window, of course. Sit down, boy.' He made a space on the table for the student waitress to put down Cornut's place-setting. The whole cloth was covered with photographic prints. He handed one to Cornut. 'Tell me,' he said apologetically, 'does that look like a picture of a star to you?'

'No.' Cornut was not very interested in his department head's hobbies. The print looked like a light-struck blob of nothing much at all.

Carl sighed and put it down. 'All right. Now, what about this thing this morning?'

Cornut accepted a cup of coffee from one of the student waitresses and waved away the others. 'I wish I could,' he said seriously.

Carl waited.

'I mean – it's hard.'

Carl waited.

Cornut took a long swallow of coffee and put down his cup. Carl was probably the only man on the faculty who hadn't been listening to the grapevine that morning. It was almost impossible to say to him the simple fact of what had happened. Master Carl was a child of the University, just as Cornut himself was; like Cornut, he had been born in the University's Medical Centre and educated in the University's schools. He had no taste for the boiling, bustling Townie world outside. In fact, he had very little taste for human problems at all. Lord knew what Carl, dry as digits, his head crammed with Vinogradoff and Frénicle de Bessy, would make of so non-mathematical a phenomenon as suicide.

'I've tried to kill myself nine times,' Cornut said, plunging in, 'don't ask me why; I don't know. That's what this morning was all about. It was my ninth try.'

Master Carl's expression was fully what Cornut had anticipated.

'Don't look so incredulous,' he snapped. '*I* don't know any more about it than that. It's just as much of an annoyance to me as it is to you!'

The house-master looked helplessly at the photographic prints by his plate as though some answer might be there. It wasn't. 'All right,' he said, rubbing the lobes of bone over his eyes. 'I understand your statement. Has it occurred to you that you might get help?'

'Help? My God, I've got helpers all over the place. The thing is worst in the morning, you see; just when I'm waking up, not fully alert, that's the bad time. So I've set up a whole complicated system of alarms. I have five clocks set. I got the superintendent's office to rig up the lights on a timed switch. I got the night proctor to call me on the house phone – all of them together, you see, so that when I wake up, I wake up *totally*. It worked for three mornings, and, believe me, the only thing that that experience resembles is being awakened by a pot of ice-water in the face. I even got Egerd to come in early every morning to stand by while I woke, just on the chance that something would go wrong.'

'But this morning Egerd was late?'

'He was tardy,' Cornut corrected. 'A minute more and he would have been late. And so would I.'

Carl said, "That's not exactly the sort of help I had in mind.'

'Oh. You mean the Med Centre.' Cornut reached for a cigarette. A student waitress hurried over with a light. He knew her. She was in one of his classes; a girl named Locille. She was pretty and very young. Cornut said absently, following her with his eyes, 'I've been there, Carl. They offered me analysis. In fact, they were quite insistent.'

Master Carl's face was luminous with interest. Cornut, turning back to look at him, thought that he hadn't seen Carl quite so absorbed in anything since their last discussion about the paper Cornut was doing for him: the analysis of the discrepancies in Wolgren's basic statistical law.

Carl said, 'I'll tell you what astonishes me. You don't seem very worried about all this.'

Cornut reflected. '. . . I am, though.'

'You don't show it. Well, is there anything else that's worrying you?'

'Worrying me enough to kill myself? No. But I suppose there must be, mustn't there?'

Carl stared into the empty air. The eyes were bright blue again; Master Carl was operating with his brain, examining possibilities, considering their relevancy, evolving a theory. 'Only in the mornings?'

'Oh no, Carl. I'm much more versatile than that; I can try to kill myself at any hour of the day or night. But it happens when I'm drowsy. Going to sleep, waking up – once in the middle of the night. I found myself walking towards the fire stairs, God knows why. Perhaps something happened to half-wake me, I don't know. So I have Egerd keep me company at night until I'm thoroughly asleep, and again in the morning. My baby-sitter.'

Carl said testily, 'Surely you can tell me more than this!'

'Well. . . . Yes, I suppose I can. I think I have dreams.'

'Dreams?'

'I think so, Carl. I don't remember very well, but it's as though someone were *telling* me to do these things, someone in a position of authority. A father? I don't remember my own father, but that's the feeling I get.'

The light went out of Carl's face. He had lost interest. Cornut said curiously. 'What's the matter?'

The house-master leaned back, shaking his head. 'No, you mustn't think anyone is telling you, Cornut. There isn't anyone. I've checked it very thoroughly, believe me. Dreams come from the dreamer.'

'But I only said – '

Master Carl held up his hand. 'To consider any other possibility,' he lectured, in the voice that reached three million viewers every week, 'involves one of two possibilities. Let us examine them. First, there might be a physical explanation. That is, someone may actually be speaking to you as you sleep. I assume we can dismiss that. The second possibility is telepathy. And that,' he said sadly, 'does not exist.'

'But I only – '

'Look within yourself, my boy,' the old man said wisely. Then, his expression showing dawning interest

14

again, 'And what about Wolgren? Any progress with the anomalies?'

Twenty minutes later, on the plea that he was late for an appointment, Cornut made his escape. There were twelve tables in the room, and he was invited to sit down at eight of them for a second cup of coffee . . . and, oh yes, what *is* this story all about, Cornut?

His appointment, although he hadn't said so to Master Carl, was with his analyst. Cornut was anxious to keep it.

He wasn't very confident of analysis as a solution to his problem; despite three centuries, the technique of mental health had never evolved a rigorous proof system, and Cornut was innately sceptical of whatever was not susceptible of mathematical analysis. But there was something else he had neglected to tell Master Carl.

Cornut was not the only one of his kind.

The man at the Med Centre had been quite excited. He named five names that Cornut recognized, faculty members who had killed themselves or died in ambiguous circumstances within the past few years. One had made fifteen attempts before he finally succeeded in blowing himself up after an all-night polymerization experiment in the Chem Hall. A couple had succeeded on the first or second try.

What made Cornut exceptional was that he had got through seven weeks of this without even seriously maiming himself. The all-time record was ten weeks. That was the chemist.

The analyst had promised to have all the information about the other suiciders to show him this morning. Cornut could not deny that he was interested. Indeed, it was a matter of considerable concern.

Unless all precedent was wrong, he would succeed as

all the others had ultimately succeeded; he would kill himself one way or another, and he probably never would know why he had done it.

And unless precedent was wrong again, it would happen within the next three weeks.

Chapter Three

The University was beginning its day. In the Regents Office a clerk filled a hopper and flipped a switch, and Sticky Dick – sometimes written as S. T.-I. (C.E.), Di. C. – began to grind out grades on the previous day's examinations in English, Sanskrit and the nuclear reactions of the Bethe Phoenix cycle. Student orderlies in Med School wheeled their sectioned cadavers out of the refrigerated filing-drawers, playing the time-honoured ribald jokes with the detached parts. In the central tape room, the TV technicians went about their endless arcane ritual of testing circuits and balancing voltages; every lecture was put on tape as a matter of course, even those which were not either broadcast or syndicated.

Thirty thousand undergraduates ran hastily over the probable mood of their various instructors, and came to the conclusion that they would be lucky to live through to evening. But it was better than trying to get along in the outside world, all the same.

And in the kitchen attached to the faculty dining-room of Math Tower the student waitress, Locille, helped her C. E. mop the last drops of damp off the stainless steel cooking utensils. She hung up her apron, checked her make-up in the mirror by the door, descended in the service elevator and went out to the hot, loud walks of the Quad.

Locille didn't think them either hot or loud. She had known much worse.

Locille was a scholarship girl; her parents were Town, not Gown. She had only been at the University for two years. She still spent some of her weekends at home. She knew very clearly what it was like to live in the city across the bay – or worse, to live on one of the texases off the coast – with your whole life a rattling, banging clamour day and night and everyone piled up against everyone else. The noise in the Quadrangle was only human voices. The ground did not shake.

Locille had a happy small face, short hair, a forthright way of walking out. She did not look worried but she was. He had looked so *tired* this morning! Also he wasn't eating, and that was not like him. If it wasn't scrambled eggs and bacon it was a hot cereal with fruit on top, always. Instinctively she approved of a man who ate well. Perhaps, she planned, smiling at a boy who greeted her without really seeing his face at all, tomorrow she would just bring the scrambled eggs and put them in front of him. Probably he'd eat them.

Of course, that wasn't getting at the real problem.

Locille shivered. She felt quite helpless. It was distressing to care so much what happened to someone, and be so far outside the situation itself. . . .

Running footsteps came up behind her and slowed.

'Hi,' panted her most regular date, Egerd, falling into step. 'Why didn't you wait at the door? What about Saturday night?'

'Oh, hello. I don't know yet. They might need me at the faculty dance.'

Egerd said brusquely, 'Tell them you can't make it. You have to go out to the texas. Your brother had, uh, some disease or other, and your mother needs you to help take care of him.'

Locille laughed.

'Aw look. I've got Carnegan's boat for the evening! We can go clear down to the Hook.'

Locille cheerfully let him take her hand. She liked Egerd. He was a good-looking boy, and he was kind. He reminded her of her brother . . . well, not of her real, living brother; but of the brother she should have had. She liked Egerd. But she didn't *like* him. The distinction was quite clear in her mind. Egerd, for example, obviously *liked* her.

Egerd said, 'Well, you don't have to make up your mind now. I'll ask you again tomorrow.' That was a salesman's instinct operating; it was always better to leave the prospect with a 'maybe' than a 'no.' He guided her between two tall buildings towards the back gardens of the campus, where Agronomy had made a little Japanese retreat in the middle of fifteen intensively farmed acres of experimental peas and wheat. 'I think I got some demerits from old Carl this morning,' he said gloomily, remembering.

'Too bad,' Locille said, although that was not an unusual phenomenon. But then he caught her attention.

'I was just trying to do Cornut a favour. Trying? Hell, I saved his life.' She was all attention now. He went on, 'He was practically out the window. Loopy! You know, I think half of these professors are off their rockers – Anyway, if I hadn't got there when I did he would've been dead. *Splop*. All over the Quad.

'At that,' he said cheerfully, 'I was kind of late.'

'Egerd!'

He stopped and looked at her. 'What's the matter?'

She raged, 'You shouldn't have been late! Didn't you know Master Cornut was relying on you? Really, you ought to be more careful.'

She was actually angry. Egerd studied her thoughtfully, and stopped talking; but some of the pleasure had gone out of the morning for him. Abruptly he caught her arm.

'Locille,' he said in a completely serious tone, 'please marry me for a while. I know I'm here on a scholarship and my grades are marginal. But I won't go back. Listen, I'm not going to stay with math. I was talking to some of the fellows at Med School. There's a lot of jobs in epidemiology, and that way my math credits will do me some good. I'm not asking for ten years of your life. We can make it month to month, even, and if you don't opt for a renewal I swear I won't hold it against you. But let me try to make you want to stay with me, Locille. Please. Marry me.'

He stood looking down at her, his broad, tanned face entirely open, waiting. She didn't meet his eye.

After a moment he nodded composedly.

'All right. I can't compete with Master Cornut, can I?'

She suddenly frowned. 'Egerd, I hope you won't feel – I mean, just because you've got the idea I'm interested in Master Cornut, I hope – '

'No,' he said, grinning, 'I won't let him fall out of a window. But you know something? Pretty as you are, Locille, I don't think Cornut knows you're alive.'

The analyst followed Cornut to the door. He was furious because he hadn't got his way – not with Cornut, particularly, but furious in general. Cornut said stiffly, 'Sorry, but I *won't* put everything else aside.'

'You'll have to, if you succeed in killing yourself.'

'That's what you're supposed to prevent, isn't it? Or is this whole thing a complete waste of time?'

'It's better than killing yourself.'

Cornut shrugged. It was a logically impeccable point. The analyst wheedled. 'Won't you even stay overnight? Observation might give us the answer. . . .'

'No.'

The analyst hesitated, shrugged, shook hands. 'All right. I guess you know that if I had my way I wouldn't be asking you. I'd commit you to Med Centre.'

'Why, of course you would,' Cornut soothed. 'But you don't have your way, do you? You've undoubtedly tried to get an order from the President's Office already, haven't you?'

The analyst had the grace to look embarrassed. 'Front office interference,' he growled, 'you'd think they'd understand that Mental Health needs a *little* co-operation once in a while. . . .'

Cornut left him still muttering. As he stepped out on to the Quad the heat and noise struck him like a fist. He didn't mind, either; he was used to it.

He had recovered enough to think of the morning's escape with amusement. The feeling was wry, with a taste of worry to it, but he was able to see the funny side of it. And it was ridiculous, no doubt about it. Suicide! Miserable people committed suicide, not happy ones. Cornut was a perfectly happy man.

Even the analyst had as much as admitted that. It had been a total waste of time, making him dig and dig into his cloudy childhood recollections for some early, abscessed wound of the mind that was pouring poisons out of its secret hiding place. He didn't have any! How could he? He was Gown. His parents had been on the faculty of this very University. Before he could walk, he was given over to the crèches and the playschools, run by the best-trained experts in the world, organized according to the best principles of child guidance. Every child had love and security, every child had what the greatest minds in pediatric psychology prescribed. Trauma? There simply could not be any!

Not only was it impossible on the face of it, but Cornut's whole personality showed no sign of such a thing. He enjoyed his work very much, and although he knew there was something he lacked – a secure, certain love – he also felt that in time he would have it. It did not occur to him to attempt to hurry it along.

'Good morning, good morning,' he said civilly to the knots of undergraduates on the walks. He began to whistle one of Carl's mnemonic songs. The under-graduates who nodded to him smiled. Cornut was a popular professor.

He passed the Hall of Humanities, the Lit Building, Pre-Med and the Administration Tower. As he got farther from home ground, the number of students who greeted him became smaller, but they still nodded politely to the master's cloak. Overhead the shriek of distant passing aircraft filled the sky.

The great steel sweep of the Bay Bridge was behind him, but he could still hear the unending rush of cars across it and, farther and louder, the mumble of the city.

Cornut paused at the door of the studio where he was to deliver his first lecture.

He glanced across the narrow strait at the city, where people lived who did not study. There was a mystery. It was, he thought, a problem greater than the silent murderer in his own brain. But it was not a problem he would ever have to solve.

'A good teacher is a good make-up man.' That was one of Master Carl's maxims. Cornut sat down at the long table and methodically applied a daub of neutral-coloured base to each cheekbone. The camera crew began sighting in on him as he worked the cream into his skin, down from the bone and away.

'Need any help?' Cornut looked up and greeted his producer.

'No thanks.' He brought the corners of his eyebrows down a fraction of an inch.

The clock was clicking off half-seconds. Cornut pencilled in age-lines (that was the price you paid for being a full professor at thirty) and brushed on the lip colour. He leaned forward to examine himself more closely in the mirror, but the producer stopped him. 'Just a minute – Dammit, man, not so much red!'

The cameraman turned a dial; in the monitor, Cornut's image appeared a touch paler, a touch greener.

'That's better. All done, professor?'

Cornut wiped his fingers on a tissue and set the golden wig on his head. 'All done,' he said, rising just as the minute hand touched the hour of ten.

From a grill at the top of the screen that dominated the front of the studio came the sounds of his theme music, muted for the studio audience. Cornut took his place in front of the class, bowed, nodded, smiled, and kicked at the pedal of the prompter until he found his place.

The class was full. He had more than a hundred students physically present. Cornut liked a large flesh-and-blood enrolment – because he was a traditionalist, but even more because he could tell from their faces how well he was getting across. This class was one of his favourites. They responded to his mood, but without ever overdoing. They didn't laugh too loud when he made a conventional academic joke, they didn't cough or murmur. They never distracted the attention of the huger, wider broadcast audience from himself.

Cornut looked over the class while the announcer was

finishing his remarks to the broadcast watchers. He saw Egerd, looking upset and irritable about something, whispering to the girl from the faculty dining-room. What was her name? Locille. Lucky fellow, Cornut thought absently to himself, and then the Binomial Theorem entered his mind – it was never far away – and displaced everything else.

'Good morning,' he said, 'and let's get to work. Today we're going to take up the relationship of Pascal's Triangle to the Binomial Theorem.' A sting of organ music rode in under his words. Behind him, on the monitor, the symbols $p+q$ appeared in letters of golden fire. 'I presume you all remember what the Binomial Theorem is – unless you've been cutting your classes.' Very small laugh – actually a sort of sub-aural grunt, just about what the very small jocularity deserved. 'The expansion of p plus q is, of course, its square, cube, fourth power and so on.' Behind him an invisible hand began multiplying $p+q$ by itself in bright gold. 'P plus q squared is p-squared plus two pq plus q-squared. P plus q cubed – ' The writer in gold noted the sum as he spoke: $p^3 + 3p^2q + 3pq^2 + q$.

'That's simple enough, isn't it?' He paused; then, deadpan, 'Well then, how come Sticky Dick says fifteen per cent of you missed it in the last test?' A warmer giggle, punctuated with a couple of loud, embarrassed hee-haws from the back. Oh, they were a very fine class.

The letters and numbers wiped themselves from the screen and a little red-faced comic cartoon figure of a bricklayer dropped into view and began building a pyramid of bricks:

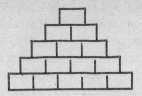

'Now, forget about the theorem for a moment – that won't be hard for some of you.' (Small giggle which he rode over.) 'Consider Pascal's Triangle. We build it just like a brick wall, only – Hold it a minute there, friend.' The cartoon bricklayer paused, and looked curiously out at the audience. 'Only we don't start from the bottom. We build it from the top down.' The cartoon bricklayer did a comic pitfall in astonishment. Then, shrugging, he got up, erased the old wall with a sweep of his trowel, hung a brick in space and began building a triangle under it.

'And we don't do it with bricks,' added Cornut. 'We do it with numbers.'

The bricklayer straightened up, kicked the wall off the screen and followed after it, pausing just at the rim of visibility to stick his tongue out at Cornut. The monitor went to a film with live models, cartwheeling into view along the banks of seats of the university's football stadium, each model carrying a placard with a number, arranging themselves in a Pascal Triangle:

$$
\begin{array}{ccccccccc}
& & & & 1 & & 1 & & \\
& & & 1 & & 2 & & 1 & \\
& & 1 & & 3 & & 3 & & 1 \\
& 1 & & 4 & & 6 & & 4 & & 1 \\
1 & & 5 & & 10 & & 10 & & 5 & & 1
\end{array}
$$

Cornut turned to relish the construction Pascal had first written down, centuries before. 'You will note,' he said, 'that each number is the sum of the two terms nearest in the line above it. The Pascal Triangle is more than a pretty pattern. It represents – ' He had them. Their faces were rapt. The class was going very well.

Cornut picked up the ivory-tipped pointer that lay on his desk, clustered with the ceremonial desk furnishings of the instructor – paper cutter, shears, pencils; all there for appearance – and with the aid of every audio-visual help possible to man, began explaining to three million viewers the relation between Pascal's Triangle and the binomial distribution.

Every line on Cornut's face, every word, every posturing ballet dancer or animated digit that showed itself on the monitor behind him, was caught in the tubes of the cameras, converted into high-frequency pulses and hurled out at the world.

Cornut had more than a hundred live watchers – the cream; the chosen ones who were allowed to attend University *in person* – but his viewers altogether numbered three million. In the relay tower at Port Monmouth a senior shift engineer named Sam Gensel watched with concentrated attention as across the dimpled tummies of the five girls in the fourth line of the Pascal Triangle electronics superimposed the symbols

$$p^4 + 4p^3q + 6p^2q^2 + 4pq^3 + q^4$$

He was not interested in the astonishing fact that the signs of the five terms in the expansion of $(p+q)^4$ were 1, 4, 6, 4 and 1 – the same as the numbers in the fourth line of the triangle – but he cared very much that the image was a trifle fuzzy. He twisted a vernier, scowled, turned it back; threw switches that called in an alternate circuit, and was rewarded by a crisper, clearer image.

At some relay point a tube was failing. He picked up the phone to call the maintenance crew.

The crisper, clearer signal was beamed up to the handiest television-relay satellite and showered back down on the world. On the Sandy Hook texas a boy named Roger Hoskins, smelling seriously of fish, paused by the door of his room to watch. He did not care about mathematics, but he was a faithful viewer, his sister was in the class, and Mom was always grateful when he could tell her that he'd caught a glimpse of their very fortunate, very seldom encountered daughter. In a crèche over lower Manhattan three toddlers munched fibrous crackers and watched; the harried nursery teacher had discovered that the moving colours kept them quiet. On the twenty-fifth floor of a tenement on Staten Island a monocar motorman named Frank Moran sat in front of his set while Cornut reviewed Pascal's thesis. Moran did not get much benefit from it. He had just come off the night shift. He was asleep.

There were many of them, the accidental or disinterested dialers-in. But there were more, there were thousands, there were uncounted hundreds of thousands who were following the proceedings with absorption.

For education was something very precious indeed.

The thirty thousand at the University were the lucky ones; they had passed the tests, stiffer every year. Not one out of a thousand passed those tests; it wasn't only a matter of intelligence, it was a matter of having the talents that could make a University education fruitful – in terms of society. For the world had to work. The world was too big to be idle. The land that had fed three billion people now had to feed twelve billion.

Cornut's television audience could, if it wished, take tests and accumulate credits. That was what Sticky Dick was for; electronically it graded papers, supplied term averages and awarded diplomas for students no professor ever saw. Almost always the credits led nowhere. But to those trapped in dreary production or drearier caretaker jobs for society, the hope was important. There was a young man named Max Steck, for example, who had already made a small contribution to the theory of normed rings. It was not enough. Sticky Dick said he would not justify a career in mathematics. He was trapped as a sex-writer, for Sticky Dick's analysers had found him prurient-minded and creative. There were thousands of Max Stecks.

Then there was Charles Bingham. He was a reactor hand at the 14th Street generating plant. Mathematics might help him, in time, become a supervising engineer. It also might not – the candidates for that job were already lined up fifty deep. But there were half a million Charles Binghams.

Sue-Ann Flood was the daughter of a farmer. Her father drove a helipopper, skimming the ploughed fields, seeding, spraying, fertilizing, and he knew that the time she put in on college-level studies would not help her gain admittance to the University. Sue-Ann knew it too; Sticky Dick measured abilities and talents, not knowledge. But she was only fourteen years old. She hoped. There were more than two million like Sue-Ann, and every one of them knew that all the others would be disappointed.

Those, the millions of them, were the invisible audience who watched Master Cornut's tiny image on a cathode screen. But there were others. One watched from Bogotà and one from Buenos Aires. One in Saskatchewan said, You goofed this morning, and one flying high over the Rockies said, Can't we try him now?

And one was propped on incredibly soft pillows in front of a set not more than a quarter of a mile from Cornut himself; and he said, It's worth a try. The son of a bitch is getting in my hair.

It was not the easiest task ever given man, to explain the relationship between the Pascal Triangle and the Binomial Distribution, but Cornut was succeeding. Master Carl's little mnemonic jingles helped, and what helped most of all was the utter joy Cornut took in it all. It was, after all, his life. As he led the class, he felt again the wonder he himself had felt, sitting in a class like this one. He hardly heard the buzz from the class as he put his pointer down to gesture, and blindly picked it up again, still talking. Teaching mathematics was a kind of hypnosis for him, an intense, gut-wrenching absorption that had gripped him from the time of his first math class. That was what Sticky Dick had measured, and that was why Cornut was a full professor at thirty. It was a wonder that so strange a thing as a number should exist in the first place, rivalled only by the greater wonder that they should perform so obediently the work of mankind.

The class buzzed and whispered.

It struck Cornut cloudily that they were whispering more than usual.

He looked up, absent-mindedly. There was an itch at the base of his throat. He scratched it with the tip of the pointer, half distracted from the point he was trying to make. But the taped visual aids on the screen were timed just so and he could not falter; he picked up the thread of what he was saying; itch and buzz faded out of his mind. . . .

Then he faltered again.

Something was wrong. The class was buzzing louder.

The students in the first row were staring at him with a unanimous, unprecedented expression. The itch returned compellingly. He scratched at it; it still itched; he dug at it with the pointer.

– No. Not with the pointer. Funny, he thought, there was the pointer on his desk.

Suddenly his throat hurt very much.

'Master Cornut, stop!' screamed someone – a girl. . . . Tardily he recognized the voice, Locille's voice, as she leaped to her feet, and half the class with her. His throat was a quick deep pain, like fire. A warm tickling thread slipped across his chest – blood! From his throat! He stared at the thing in his hand, and it was not the pointer at all but the letter-opener, steel and sharp. Confused and panicked, he wheeled to gaze at the monitor. There was his own face, over a throat that bore a narrow trickling slash of blood!

Three million viewers gasped. Half the studio class was boiling towards him, Egerd and the girl ahead of the rest. 'Easy, sir! Here, let me –' That was Egerd, with a tissue, pressing it against the wound. 'You'll be all right, sir! It's only – But it was close!'

Close. . . . He had all but cut his jugular vein in two, right in front of his class and the watching world. The murderer inside his head was getting very strong and sure, to brave the light of day.

Chapter Four

Cornut was literally a marked man now. He had a neat white sterile bandage on his throat, and the medics had cheerfully assured him that when the bandage was gone there would be a handsome scar. They demanded that he stay around for a complete psychomedical checkup. He said no. They said Would you rather be dead? He said he wasn't going to die. They said How can you be sure? But, as it turned out, the clinic was not going to be free for that sort of thing for a couple of hours, and he fought his way free. He was extremely angry at the medics for annoying him, at himself for being such a fool, at Egerd for staunching the flow of his blood, at Locille for seeing it . . . his patience was exhausted with the world.

Cornut strode like a blinkered cart-horse to the Math Tower gym, looking neither to left nor right, though he knew what he would see. Eyes. The eyes of everyone on the campus, looking at him and whispering. He found an undergraduate who was reasonably willing to mind his own business (the boy only looked slightly doubtful when Cornut chose his épée, but one glimpse of Cornut's face made his own turn into opaque stone), and they two fenced for a furious half-hour. The medics had told Cornut to be sure to rest. Winded and muscles aching, he returned to his room to do so.

He spent a long, thoughtful afternoon lying on his bed

and looking at the ceiling, but nothing came of it. The whole thing was simply too irritating to be borne.

Medics or not, at a quarter to five he put on a clean shirt to keep his appointment at the faculty tea.

The tea was a sort of official send-off to the University's Field Expedition. Attendance was compulsory, especially for those who, like Cornut, were supposed to make the trip; but that was not why he was there. He considered it to be his last good chance to get off the list.

There were three hundred persons in the huge, vaulted room. The University conspicuously consumed space; it was a tradition, like the marginal pencillings in all the books in the library. Every one of the three hundred glanced once quickly at Cornut as he came in, then away – some with a muffled laugh, some with sympathy, the worst with an unnatural lack of any expression at all. So much for the grapevine. Damn them, Cornut thought bitterly, you'd think no professor ever tried to commit suicide before. He couldn't help overhearing some of the whispers.

'And that's the *seventh* time. It's because he's *desperate* to be department head and old Carl *won't* step down.'

'Esmeralda! You know you're making that up!'

His face flaming, Cornut walked briskly past the little knot. It was like a fakir's bed of coals; every step seemed to crisp him. But there were other things to gossip about at the tea, and some of the captured fragments of talk did not concern him at all.

' – want us to get along with a fourteen-year-old trevatron. You know what the China's have? Six brand-new ones. *And* coin silver for the windings!'

'Yes, but there's two billion of them. Per capita we stack up pretty – '

Cornut halted in the middle of the drinking, eating, talking, surging mass and looked about for Master Carl. He caught sight of him. The department head was paying his respects to a queer-looking, ancient figure – St Cyr, the President of the University. Cornut was startled. St Cyr was an old man and by his appearance a sick one; it was rare to see him at a faculty tea. Still, this one was special – and anyway, that could make it a lot easier to get off the list.

Cornut pushed his way towards them, past a stocky drunk from humanities who was whispering ribaldly to a patient student waitress, and threaded his way through a group of anatomists from the med school.

'Notice what decent cadavers we've been getting lately? It hasn't been this good since the last shooting war. Of course, they're not much good except for geriatrics, but that's selective euthanasia for you.'

'Will you watch what you're doing with that Martini?'

Cornut made his way slowly towards Master Carl and President St Cyr. The closer he got, the easier it was to move. There were fewer people at St Cyr's end of the room; he was the central figure of the gathering, but the guests did not cluster around him; that's the kind of a man he was.

The kind of a man St Cyr was was this: He was the ugliest man in the room.

There were others who were in no way handsome – old, or fat, or sick. St Cyr was something special. His face was an artifact of ugliness. Deep old scars made a net across his face like the flimsy cloth that holds a cheese. Surgery? No one knew. He had always had them. And his skin was a cyanotic blue.

Master Greenlease (physical chem) and Master Wahl (anthropology) were there, Wahl because he was too drunk to care who he spoke to, no doubt; Greenlease because Carl had him by the elbow and would not let him go. St Cyr nodded four times at Cornut, like a pendulum. 'Nice wea-ther,' he said, rolling it like a clock.

'Yes, it is, sir. Excuse me. Carl – '

St Cyr lifted the hand that hung by his side and laid it limply in Cornut's hand – it was his version of a handshake. He opened his seamed mouth and gave the series of unvoiced glottal stops that were his version of a chuckle. 'It will be heav-y weath-er for Mas-ter Wahl,' he said, spacing out the syllables like an articulate metronome. It was his version of a joke.

Cornut gave him a waxen smile and a small waxen laugh. The reference was to the fact that Wahl, too, was scheduled to go on the Field Expedition. Cornut didn't think that was funny – not as far as he himself was concerned, anyway – not when he had so many other things on his mind.

'Carl,' he said, 'excuse me.' But Master Carl had other things on his mind; he was badgering Greenlease for information about molecular structure, heaven knew why. And also St Cyr had not released his hand.

Cornut grumbled internally and waited. Wahl was giggling over some involved faculty joke to which St Cyr was listening like a judge. Cornut spared himself the annoyance of listening to it and thought about St Cyr. Queer old duck, of course. That was where you started. You could account for some of the queerness by, say, a bad heart. That would be the reason for the blueness. But what would be the reason for not having it operated on?

And then, what about the other things? The deadpan expression. The lifeless voice, with its firmly pronounced terminal 'ings' and words without a stress syllable anywhere? St Cyr talked like a clockwork man. Or a deaf one?

But again, what would be the reason for a man allowing himself to be deaf?

Especially a man who owned a University, *including* an 800-bed teaching hospital.

Wahl at last noticed that Cornut was present and punched his shoulder – cordially, Cornut decided, after thought. 'Committed any good suicides lately, boy?' He hiccoughed. 'Don't blame you. Your fault, President, you know, dragging him off to Tahiti with us. He doesn't *like* Tahiti.'

Cornut said, with control, 'The Field Expedition isn't going to Tahiti.'

Wahl shrugged. 'The way us anthropologists look at it, one gook island is like another gook island.' He even made a joke of his specialty! Cornut was appalled.

On the other hand, St Cyr seemed neither to notice nor to mind. He flopped his hand free of Cornut's and rested it casually on Wahl's weaving shoulder. The other hand held the full highball glass which, Cornut had observed, always remained full. St Cyr did not drink or smoke (not even tobacco), nor had Cornut ever seen him give a second look to a pretty girl. 'Lis-ten,' he said in his slow-march voice, turning Wahl to face Carl and the chemist. 'This is in-ter-est-ing.'

Carl was oblivious of the President, of Cornut, of everything except the fact that the chemist by his side knew something that Carl himself wanted to know. The information was there; he went after it. 'I don't seem to make myself clear. What I want to know, Greenlease, is how I can visualize the exact *structure* of a molecule. Do you follow me? For example, what *colour* is it?'

The chemist looked uncomfortably at St Cyr, but St Cyr was apparently absorbed. 'Well,' he said. 'Uh. The concept of colour doesn't apply. Light waves are too long.'

'Ah! I see.' Carl was fascinated. 'Well, what about the shape? I've seen those tinker-toy constructions. The atoms are little balls and they're held together with plastic rods – I suppose they represent connecting force. Are they anything like the real thing?'

'Not much. The connecting force is real enough, but you can't see it – or maybe you could, at that' (Greenlease, like most of the faculty members present, had had a bit more than enough; he was not of a temper to try to interpret molecular forces in tinker-toy terms for professors who, whatever their status in Number Theory, were physical-chemical idiots) 'if, that is, you could see the atoms in the first place. One is no more impossible than the other. But the connecting force would not look like a rod, any more than the gravitation that holds the moon to the earth would look like a rod. . . . Let's see. . . . Do you know what I mean by the word "valence"? No. Well, do you know enough atomic theory to know what part is played by the number of electrons in – Or, look at it a different way.' He paused. By his expression, he was getting seriously annoyed, in a way he considered unjust – like an ivory hunter who, carrying a .400 Express in his crooked arm, cannot quite see how to cope with the attack of a hungry mosquito. He seemed on the point of reviewing atomic structure back through Bohr and well on the way to Democritus. 'I'll tell you what,' he said at last, 'stop around tomorrow if you can. I have

36

some plates made under the electron microscope.'

'Oh, thank you!' cried Carl with enthusiasm. 'Tomorrow – but tomorrow I'll be off on this con—' he. smiled at St Cyr – 'tomorrow I'll be with the Field Expedition. Well, as soon as I get back, Greenlease. Don't forget.' He warmly shook hands as the chemist took his leave.

Cornut hissed angrily. 'That's what I want to talk to you about.'

Carl looked startled but pleased. 'I didn't know you were interested in my little experiments, Cornut. That was quite fascinating. I've always thought of a molecule of silver nitrate, for example, as being black or silvery. Perhaps that's where my work has gone wrong. Greenlease says – '

'No. I'm not talking about that. I mean the Field Expedition. I *can't* go.'

An observer a yard away would have thought that all of St Cyr's attention was on Wahl; he had lost interest in the dialogue between Carl and Greenlease minutes before. But the old head turned like a parabolic mirror. The faded blue eyes radared in on Cornut. The slow metronome ticked, 'You must go, Cor-nut.'

'Must go? Of course you must go. Good heavens, Cornut – Don't mind him, President. Certainly he'll go.'

'But I have all the Wolgren to get through –'

'And then a su-i-cide to com-mit.' The muscles at the corner of the mouth tried to twitch the blue lips upwards, to show that it was a pleasantry.

But Cornut was nettled. 'Sir, I don't intend to – '

'You did not in-tend to this morn-ing.'

Carl interrupted. 'Cornut, be quiet. President, that was distressing, of course. I've had a full report on it, and

I believe we can pass it off as an accident. Perhaps it was an accident. I don't know. It would have been quite easy to pick up the paper-knife in error.'

Cornut said, 'But – '

'In an-y case, he must go.'

'Naturally, President. You understand that, don't you, Cornut?'

'But – '

'You will take the ad-vance plane, please. I want you to be there when I ar-rive.'

'Very well. It's settled, then.'

'But – ' said Cornut, but he was destined never to get a word deeper into that thought; through the mill of faculty came a man and a woman with the tense, nervous bearing of Townies. The woman carried a photo-taper; the man was a reporter from one of the nets.

'President St Cyr? Yes, of course. Thanks for inviting us. Naturally, we'll have a whole crew here when your expedition gets back, but I wonder if we can't get a few photographs now. As I understand it, you've located seven aboriginals. Seven? I see. It's a whole tribe, then, but seven are being brought back here. And who is the head of the expedition? Oh, naturally. Millie, will you be sure to get President St Cyr?'

The reporter's thumb was on the trigger of his voice-taper, getting down the fact that nine faculty members were going to bring back the seven aborigines, that the expedition would leave, in two planes, at nine o'clock that night, so as to arrive at their destination in early morning, local time; and that the benefits to anthropological research would surely be beyond calculation.

Cornut drew Master Carl aside. 'I don't want to go! What the hell does this have to do with mathematics, anyhow?'

'Now, please, Cornut. You heard the President. It has nothing to do with mathematics, no, but it is purely a ceremonial function and a good deal of an honour. At the present time, you should not refuse it. You can see that some rumours of your, uh, accidents have reached him. Don't cause friction.'

'What about the Wolgren? What about my, uh, accidents? Even here I nearly kill myself, and I'm all set up. What will I do without Egerd?'

'I'll be with you.'

'No, Carl!'

Carl said, speaking very clearly, 'You are going.' The eyes were star-sapphires.

Cornut studied the eyes for a moment, and then gave up. When Carl got that expression and that tone of voice, it meant that argument served no further useful purpose. Since Cornut loved the old man, he always stopped arguing at that point.

'I'm going,' he said. But the expression on his face would have soured wine.

Cornut packed – it took five minutes – and went back to the clinic to see if diagnostic space was free. It was not. He was cutting his time very close – take-off for the first plane was in less than an hour – but mulishly he took a seat in the reception room. Stolidly he did not look at the clock.

When the examination room was available things went briskly. His vital statistics were machine-measured and machine-studied, his blood spectrum was machine-chromatographed, automatically the examining table was tipped so that he could step off, and as he dressed a photoelectric eye behind his hanging garments glanced at him, opened the door to the outside corridor and said,

'Thank you. Wait in the outer office, please,' from a machine-operated tape.

Master Carl, in a fluster, found him waiting.

'Good God, boy! Do you know the plane's about to take off? And the President *specially* said we were to go in the first plane. Come on! I've a scooter waiting. . . .'

'Sorry.'

'Sorry? What the devil do you mean, sorry? Come!'

Cornut said flatly, 'I agreed to go. I will go. But, as there is some feeling, shared by yourself, that the medics can help keep me from killing myself, I do not intend to leave this building until they tell me what I must do. I am waiting for the results of my examination now.'

Master Carl said, 'Oh.' He glanced at the clock on the wall. 'I see,' he said. He sat down beside Cornut thoughtfully.

Suddenly he grinned. 'All right, boy. The President can't argue with that.'

Cornut relaxed. He said, 'Well, you go ahead, Carl. No reason for both of us to get in trouble – '

'Trouble!' Master Carl seemed quite gay. Cornut realized that it had finally occurred to the house-master that this trip was a sort of vacation; he was practising for a holiday mood. 'Why should there be any trouble? You have a good reason for being tardy. I, too, have a good reason for waiting for you. After all, the President urged me to bring the Wolgren analysis along. He's quite interested, you know. And as I did not see it in your room, I suppose it is in your bags; therefore I will wait for your bags.'

Cornut protested, 'But it isn't anywhere near finished!'

Carl actually winked. 'Now, do you suppose he'll

know the difference? Be flattered that he is interested enough to pretend to look at it!'

Cornut said grudgingly, 'Well, all right. How the devil did he hear about it in the first place?'

'I told him, of course. I – I've had occasion to discuss you with him a good deal, these past few days.' Carl's expression lost some of its glow. 'Cornut,' he said severely, 'we can't let this go on, can we? You must regularize your life. Take a woman.'

Cornut exploded, 'Master Carl! You have no *right* to interfere in my personal affairs!'

'Trust me, boy,' the old man wheedled. 'This thing with Egerd is only a makeshift. A thirty-day marriage would surely see you through the worst of it, wouldn't it?'

Three weeks, thought Cornut, diverted.

'And, truly, you need a wife. It is bad for a man to go through life alone,' he explained.

Cornut snapped, 'How about you?'

'I'm older. You're young. How long is it since you've had a wife.'

Cornut was obstinately silent.

'You see? There are many lovely young girls in the University. They would be proud. Any of them.'

Cornut did not want his mind to roam the corridors that had just been opened for it, but it did.

'Besides, you will have her with you at all the dangerous times. You won't need Egerd.'

Cornut's mind ran back quickly and began to trace a more familiar, less attractive maze. 'I'll think about it,' he said at last, just as the medic came in with his report, a couple of boxes of pills and a sheaf of papers. The report was negative, all down the line. The pills? They were just in case, said the medic; they couldn't hurt, they might help.

And the sheaf of papers. ... The top one said:

Confidential. Tentative. Studies of Suicidal Tendencies in Faculty Members.

Cornut covered it with his hand, interrupted the medic as he was about to explain the delay in getting the dossiers for him and cried, 'Let's get a move on, Carl! We can still make that plane.'

But, as it turned out, they couldn't.

As fast as the scooter would go, they got to the aircraft park just in time to see the first section of the Field Expedition lift itself off the ground with a great whistling roar on its V T O jets.

Much to Cornut's surprise, Master Carl was not upset. 'Oh, well,' he said, 'we had our reasons. It isn't as though we were *arbitrarily* late. And anyway –' he allowed himself another wink, the second in a quarter of an hour – 'this gives us a chance to ride in the President's private plane, eh? Real living for us of the under-privileged class!' He even opened his mouth to chuckle, but he didn't do it, or if he did the sound was not heard. Overhead there was a gruff giant's cough and a bright spray of flame. They looked up. Flame, flame all over the heavens, falling in great white droplets to the earth.

'My God,' said Cornut softly, 'and that was our plane.'

Chapter Five

'Nothing loath,' said Master Carl thoughtfully, 'I kissed your concubine.' He squinted out of the window of the jet, savouring the sentence. It was good. Yes. But was it perfect?

A towering cumulo-nimbus, far below, caught his attention and distracted him. He sighed. He didn't feel like working. Apparently everyone else in the jet was asleep. Or pretending to be. Only St Cyr, way up in front, propped on pneumatic pillows in the semi-circular lounge, looked as much awake as he ever did. But it was better not to talk to St Cyr. Carl was aware that most conversations involving himself turned, sooner or later, to either his private researches or to Number Theory. As he knew more about either than anyone else alive, they wound up as lectures. That was no good with St Cyr. He had made it clear long ago that he was not interested in being instructed by the instructors he hired.

Also he was in a bad mood.

It was odd, thought Master Carl, less in resentment than in a spirit of scientific inquiry, but St Cyr had been quite furious with Cornut and himself for no good reason. It could not have been for missing the first plane – if they'd caught it, they would have died, just like its crew and the four graduate students it carried. But St Cyr had been furious, the tick-tock voice hoarse and breathless, the hairless eyebrows almost scowling. Master Carl took his eyes away from the window and abandoned the question of St Cyr. Let him sulk. Carl didn't like problems that had no solution. *Nothing loath, I kissed your concubine.* But mightn't it be better to stick to song-writing?

He became conscious of a beery breath on the back of his neck.

'I'm glad you're awake, Wahl,' he said, turning, his face inches away from the hung-over face of the anthropologist. 'Let me have your opinion, please. Which is easier to remember: "Nothing loath, I kissed your concubine." Or, "Last digit? O, a potential square!" '

Wahl shuddered. 'For God's sake. I just woke up.'

'Why, I don't think that matters. It might help. The whole idea is to present the mnemonic in a form that is available under any conditions – including,' he said delicately, 'a digestive upset.' He rotated his chair to face Wahl, flipping through his notebook to display a scribbled page. 'Can you read that? The idea, you see, is to provide a handy recognition feature for quick factoring of aliquot numbers. Now, you know, of course, that all squares can end in only one of six digits. No square can end in two, three, seven or eight. So my first idea – I'm still not sure that I wasn't on the right track – was to use, "No, quantity not squared." You see the utility, I'm sure. Two letters in the first word, 'no.' Eight letters in "quantity," three in "not" and seven in "squared." It's easy to remember, I think, and it's self-defining. I consider that a major advantage.'

'Oh, it is,' said Wahl.

'But,' Carl went on, 'it's negative. Also there is the chance that "no" can be misread for "nought" or "nothing" – meaning zero. So I tried the reverse approach. A square *can* end in zero, one, four, five, six or nine. Letting the ejaculative "O" stand for "zero," I then wrote: "Last digit? O, a potential square." Four, five, zero, one, nine and six – you see that. Excuse me. I'm so used to lecturing to undergraduates that sometimes I tend to over explain. But, although that has a lot to recommend it, it doesn't have – well – *yumph.*' He smiled with a touch of embarrassment. 'So, just on an inspiration, I came up with "Nothing loath, I kissed your concubine." Rather mnemonic, at least?'

'It's all of that, Carl,' agreed Wahl, rubbing his temples. 'Say, where's Cornut?'

'You realize that the "nothing," again, is "zero".'

'Oh, there he is. Hey, Cornut!'

'Be quiet! Let the boy sleep!' Carl was jolted out of his concentration. He leaned forward to see into the wing-backed seat ahead of him and was gratified to see that Cornut was still snoring faintly.

Wahl burst into a laugh, stopped abruptly with a look of surprise and clutched his head. After a moment he said, 'You take care of him like he was your baby.'

'There is no need to take that sort of – '

'Some baby! I've heard of accident-prones, but this one's fantastic. Not even Joe Btfsk wrecks planes that he ought to be in but isn't!'

Master Carl bit back his instinctive rejoinder, paused to regain his temper and pondered an appropriate remark. He was saved the trouble. The jet lurched slightly and the distant thunderheads began to wheel towards the horizon. It wasn't the clouds, of course. It was the jet swinging in for a landing, vectored by unseen radar. It was only a very small motion, but it sent Wahl lurching frantically to the washroom and it woke Master Cornut. Carl leaped up as soon as he saw the younger man move, standing over him until his eyes were open. 'Are you all right?' he demanded at once.

Cornut blinked, yawned and stretched his muscles.

– 'I guess so. Yes.'

'We're about to land.' There was relief in Carl's voice. He had not expected anything to happen. Why should it? But there had been the chance that something might. . . . 'I can get you a cup of coffee from the galley.'

'All right – no. Never mind. We'll be down in a minute.'

Below them the island was slipping back and forth slantwise, like a falling leaf – a leaf that was falling upwards, at least in their eyes, because it was growing enormously fast. Wahl came out of the washroom and stared at the houses.

'Dirty hovels,' he growled. It was raining beneath their plane – no, around them – no, over. They were through the patchy cloud layer, and the 'hovels' Wahl had glimpsed were clear beneath. Out of the patches of clouds rain was falling.

'Cum-u-lus of or-o-graph-ic or-i-gin,' said St Cyr's uninflected voice, next to Master Carl's ear. 'There is al-ways cloud at the is-land. I hope the storm does not dis-turb you.'

Master Wahl said, 'It disturbs *me*.'

They landed, the jet's wheels screaming thinly as they touched the wet concrete runway. A short, dark man with an umbrella ran out and, holding it protectively over St Cyr's head, escorted them to the administration building, though the rain had nearly stopped.

It was evident that St Cyr's reputation and standing were working for them. The whole party was passed through customs under seal; the brown-skinned inspectors didn't even touch the bags. One of them prowled briefly around the stack of the Field Expedition's luggage, carrying a portable voice-taper. 'Research instruments,' he chanted, singsong, and the machine clacked out its entry. 'Research instruments.... Research instruments.'

Master Carl interrupted, 'That's my personal bag! There aren't any research instruments in it.'

'Excuse,' said the inspector politely; but he went right on with calling every bag 'research instruments'; the only concession he made to Carl's correction was to lower his voice.

It was, to Master Carl, an offensive performance, and he had it in his mind to speak to someone in authority about it, too. Research instruments! They had nothing resembling a research instrument to their names, unless you counted the collection of handcuffs Master Wahl had brought along, just in case the aboriginals were obstinate about coming along. He thought of bringing it up to St Cyr, but the President was talking to Cornut. Carl didn't want to interrupt. He had no objection to interrupting Cornut, of course, but interrupting the President of the University was something else again.

Wahl said, 'What's that over there? Looks like a bar, doesn't it? How about a drink?'

Carl shook his head frostily and stomped out into the street. He was not enjoying his trip, and it was a pity, he thought, because he realized that he had been rather looking forward to it. One needed a change of scene from the Halls of Academe every once in a while. Otherwise one tended to become stuffy and provincial, to lose contact with the mass of humanity outside the University walls. For that reason Carl had made it a practice, through the thirty-odd years since he began to teach, at least once in every year to accept or invent some task that would bring him in contact with the non-academic world. ... They had all been quite as distasteful as this one, but since Master Carl had never realized this before it hadn't mattered.

He stood in a doorway, out of the fresh hot sun, looking down a broad street. The 'filthy hovels' were not filthy at all; it was only Wahl's bad temper that had said that, not his reason. Why, they were quite clean, Master Carl marvelled. Not *attractive*. And not *large*. But they did have a quaint and not too repulsive appearance. They were clumsy prefabs of some sort of pressed fibre, plastic bonded – a local product most likely, Master Carl diagnosed; pulp from palm trees had gone into the making of them.

A roadable helipopper whirred, dipped, settled in the street before him, folded its vanes and rolled up to the entrance of the building where Carl was standing. The driver jumped out, ran around the side of the craft and opened the door.

Now, that was odd.

The driver acted as though the Empress Catherine was about to set foot on the soil she ruled, and yet what came out of the popper was no great lady but what seemed, at least at first glance, like a fourteen-year-old blonde. Carl pursed his thin lips and squinted into the bright sun. Curious, he marvelled, the creature was waving at him!

The creature said, in a brassy voice of no fourteen-year-old, 'You're Carl. Come on, get in. I've been waiting for you people for an hour and a half, and I've got to get clear back to Rio de Janeiro tonight. And hurry up that old goat St Cyr, will you?'

To Carl's surprise, St Cyr didn't strike the child dead.

He came out and greeted her as affably as his corpse's voice could be made to sound, and he sat beside her in the front seat of the popper in the wordless association of old friends. But it wasn't the only surprising thing. Looking a little more closely at the 'girl' was a kind of surprise too, because a girl she was not. She was a painted grandmother with a face-lift, Bermuda shorts and a blonde bob! Why couldn't the woman grow old gracefully, like St Cyr, or for that matter like Master Carl himself?

All the same, if St Cyr knew her she couldn't be *all* bad, and anyway Carl had something else bothering him. Cornut was missing.

The helipopper was already on the bounce. Carl stood up. 'Wait! We're missing someone.' No one was listening. The grandmother in shorts was chattering away in St Cyr's ear, her voice queer and muffled under the sound of the sequenced rockets that whirled the vanes. 'President St Cyr! Please have this pilot turn back.' But St Cyr didn't even turn his head.

Master Carl was worried. He pressed his face to the window, looking back towards the native town, but already it was too far to see anything.

Of course, he told himself, there was no danger. There were no hostile natives anywhere in the world. Lightning would not strike. Cornut was as safe as if he were in his own bed.

– Exactly as safe, his own mind assured him sternly, but no safer.

But the fact of the matter was that Cornut was drinking a glass of beer at a dusty sidewalk table. For the first time in – was it for ever? – his mind was at rest.

He was not thinking of the anomalies a statistical census had discovered in Wolgren's Distributive Law. He was not thinking of Master Carl's suggestion about term marriage, or even about the annoying interruption that this expedition represented. It did not seem quite as much of an annoyance, now that he was here. It was so *quiet*. It was like the fragrance of a new flower. He tested it experimentally with his ears and decided that, though odd, it was pleasant. A few hundred yards away some aircraft chugged into the sky, destroying the quiet, but the odd thing was that the quiet returned.

Cornut now had the chance he had been looking for since leaving the clinic, the night before and ten thousand miles away. He ordered another beer from the sallow waitress and reached into his pocket for a sheaf of reports that medic had handed him.

There were more of them than he had expected.

How many cases had the analyst said had occurred at their own University? Fifteen or so. But here were more than a hundred case histories. He scanned the summaries quickly and discovered that the problem extended beyond the University – cases from other schools, cases from outside university circles entirely. There seemed to have been a rash of them among Government employees. There was a concentration of twelve on the staff of a single television network.

He read the meaningless names and studied the almost as meaningless facts. One of the TV men had succeeded in short-circuiting a supposedly foolproof electric mattress eight times before he managed to die of it. He was happily married and about to be promoted.

'*Ancora birra?*' Cornut jumped, but it was only the waitress. 'All right – wait.' There was no sense in these continual interruptions. 'Bring me a couple of bottles and leave them.'

The sun was setting, the clouds overhead powerless to shield the island from its heat, as the horizon was bare blue. It was hot, and the beer was making him sleepy.

It occurred to him that he really ought to be making an effort to catch up with the rest of the party. It was only chance that they had gone off without him, probably Master Carl would be furious.

It also occurred to him that it was comfortable here.

On an island as small as this, he would have no trouble finding them when he wanted them. Meanwhile he still had some beer, and he had all these reports, and it did not seem particularly disturbing to him that, though he read them all from beginning to end, he still found none where the course of the syndrome had taken more than ten weeks to reach its climax. Ten weeks. He had twenty days left.

Master Carl demanded, 'Turn back! You can't leave the poor boy to die!'

St Cyr whinnied surprisingly. The woman shrilled, 'He'll be all right. What's the matter, you want to spoil his fun? Give the kid a chance to kill himself, will you?'

Carl took a deep breath. Then he started again, but it was no use, they insisted on treating the matter lightly. He slumped back in his seat and stared out of the window.

The helipopper came down in front of a building larger than most of the prefabs. It had glass in the windows, and bars over the glass. The blonde leaped up like a stick doll and shrilled, 'Everybody out! Hop to it, now, I haven't got all day.'

Carl morosely followed her into the building. He wondered how, even for a moment and at a distance, he had taken her for a child. Bright blue eyes under blonde hair, yes; but the eyes were bloodshot, the hair a yellow mop draped on a skull. Loathing her, and worrying about Cornut, he climbed a flight of steps, went through a barred door and looked into a double-barred room.

'The aborigines,' St Cyr said in his toneless voice.

It was the local jail, and it had only one cell. And that cell was packed with a dozen or more short, olive-skinned, ragged men and women. There were no children. No children, thought Master Carl petulantly, but they had been promised an entire population to select from! These were all *old*. The youngest of them seemed at least a hundred. . . .

'Ob-serve them care-ful-ly,' came St Cyr's slow voice. 'There is not a per-son there more than fif-ty years old.'

Master Carl jumped. Mind-reading again! He thought with a touch of envy how wonderful it must be to be so wise, so experienced, so all-understanding that one could know, as St Cyr knew, what another person was thinking before he spoke it aloud. It was the sort of wisdom he hoped his subordinates would attribute to him, and they didn't; and it hurt to see that in St Cyr it existed.

Master Carl roamed fretfully down the corridor, looking through electrified bars at the aborigines. A sallow fat man in flowered shorts came in through the door, bowed to the blonde woman, bowed to St Cyr, offered a slight inclination of the head to Master Carl, staring contemptuously through the others. It was an instructive demonstration of how a really adept person could single out the categories of importance of a group of strangers on first contact. 'I,' he announced, 'am your translator. You wish to speak to your aborigines, sir. Do so. The short one there, he speaks some English.'

'Thank you,' said Master Carl. The short one was a surly-looking fellow wearing much the same costume as the others. All of them were basically clad in ragged shorts and a short-sleeved jacket with an incongruous, tight-fitting collar. The clothes looked very, very old; not merely worn, but *old*. Men and women dressed alike. Only in the collars and shoulder-bars of the jackets were there any particular variations. They seemed to have military insignia to mark their ranks. One woman's collar, for example, bore a red cloth patch with a gold stripe running through it; the red was faded, the gold was soiled, but once they had been bright. Across the gold stripe was a five-pointed star of yellow cloth. The shortest of the men, the one who looked up when the translator spoke, had a red patch with much more gold on it, and with three stars of greenish, tarnished metal. Another man had a plain red patch with three cloth stars.

These three, the two men and the woman, stepped forward, placed their palms on their knees and bowed jerkily. The one with the metal stars spoke breathily, 'Tai-i Masatura-san. I captain, sir. These are of my command: Heicho Ikuri, Joto-hei Shokuto.'

Master Carl stepped back fastidiously. They *smelt!* They didn't look dirty, exactly, but their complexions were all bad – scarred and pitted and seamed, as well as sallow; and they did have a distinct sour aura of sweat hanging over them. He glanced at the interpreter. 'Captain? Is that an Army rank?'

The interpreter grinned. 'No Army now,' he said reassuringly. 'Oh, no. Long gone. But they keep military titles, you see? Father to son, father to son, like that. This fellow here, the tai-i, he tells me they are all part of Imperial Japanese Expeditionary Force which presently will make assault landing in Washington, D.C. Tai-i is captain; he is in charge of all of them, I believe. The heicho – that's the woman – is, the captain tells, a sort of junior corporal. More important than the other fellow, who is what they call a superior private.'

'I don't know what a corporal or a private is.'

'Oh, no. Who does? But to them it is important, it seems.' The translator hesitated, grinned, and wheezed: 'Also, they are related. The tai-i is daddy, the heicho is mommy, the joto-hei is son. All named Masatura-san.'

'Dirty-looking things,' Master Carl commented. 'Thank heaven I don't have to go near them.'

'Oh,' said a grave, slow voice behind him, 'but you do. Yes, you do. It is your re-spon-si-bi-li-ty, Carl. You must su-per-vise their tests by the med-ics.'

Master Carl frowned and complained, but there was no way out of it. St Cyr gave the orders, and that was the order he gave.

The medics looked over the aborigines as thoroughly as any dissecting cadavers. Medics, thought Master Carl in disgust. How can they! But they did. They had the men and women strip – flaccid breasts, sagging bellies, a terminator of deepening olive showing the transition from shade to sun at the lines marked by collars and cuffs and the hem of their shorts. Carl took as much of it as he could, and then he walked out – leaving them nakedly proud beside their rags, while the medics fussed and muttered over them like stock judges.

It was not only that he was tired of the natives – whose interest to a mathematician was not zero, no, but a quantity vanishingly small. More than that, he wanted to find Cornut.

There was a huge moon.

Carl retraced his steps to where the helipopper was casting a black silhouette on the silver dust. The pilot was half asleep on the seat, and Carl, with a force and determination previously reserved for critical letters in *Math.*

Trans., said sharply, 'Up, you. I haven't all night.' The startled pilot was airborne with his passenger before he realized that it was neither his employer, the young-old blonde, nor her equal partner, the old, old St Cyr.

By then it did not much matter. In for a penny, in for a pound; when Carl ordered him back to the town where the jet had landed, the pilot grumbled to himself but complied.

It was not hard to find where Cornut had gone. The police scooter told Carl about the sidewalk café, the cashier told him about the native cafeteria, the counter-man had watched Cornut, failing to finish his sandwich and coffee, stagger back to – the airport again. There the traffic tower had seen him come in, try to get transportation to follow the others, fail and mulishly stagger off into the jungle on the level truck road.

He had been hardly able to keep his eyes open, the towerman added.

Carl pressed the police into service. He was frightened.

The little scooter bounced along the road, twin spotlights scanning the growth on both sides. Please don't find him, begged Carl silently. I *promised* him. . . .

The brakes squealed and the scooter skidded to a halt.

The police were small, thin, young and agile, but Master Carl was first off the scooter and first to the side of the huddled figure under the breadfruit tree.

For the first time in weeks, Cornut had fallen asleep – passed out, in fact – without a guardian angel. The moment of helplessness between waking and sleeping, the moment that had almost killed him a dozen times, had caught him by the side of a deserted road, in the middle of an uninhabited sink of smelly soft vegetation.

Carl gently lifted the limp head.

'. . . My God,' he said, a prayer instead of an oath,

'he's only drunk. Come on, you! Help me get him to bed.'

Cornut woke up with a sick mouth and a banging head, very cheerful. Master Carl was seated at a field desk, a shaded light over his head. 'Oh, you're up. Good. I had the porter call me a few minutes early, in case –'

'Yes. Thanks.' Cornut waggled his jaw experimentally, but that was not a very good experiment. Still, he felt very good. He had not been drunk in a long, long time, and a hangover was strange enough to him to be interesting in itself. He sat on the side of the bed. The porter had evidently had other orders from Master Carl, because there was coffee in a pewter pot, and a thick pottery cup. He drank some.

Carl watched him for a while, then browsed back to his desk. He had a jar of some faintly greenish liquid and the usual stack of photographic prints. 'How about this one?' he demanded. 'Does it look like a star to you?'

'No.'

Carl dropped it back on the heap. 'Becquerel's was no better,' he said cryptically.

'I'm sorry, Carl,' Cornut said cheerfully. 'You know I don't take much interest in psion –'

'Cornut!'

'Oh, sorry. In your researches into paranormal kinetics, then.'

Carl said doubtfully, having already forgotten what Cornut had said, 'I thought Greenlease had put me on the track of something. You know I've been trying to manipulate single molecules by P.K. – using photographic film, on the principle that as the molecules are just about to flip over into another state, not much energy should be needed to trigger them – Yes. Well,

Greenlease told me about Brownian Movement. Like this.' He held the jar of soap solution to the light. 'See?'

Cornut got up and took the quart jar from Master Carl's hand. In the light he could see that the greenish colour was the sum of a myriad wandering points of light, looking more gold than green. 'Brownian Movement? I remember something about it.'

'The actual motion of molecules,' Carl said solemnly. 'One molecule impinging on another, knocking it into a third, the third knocking it into a fourth. There's a term for it in –'

'In math, of course. Why, certainly. The Drunkard's Walk.' Cornut remembered the concept with clarity and affection. He had been a second-year student, and the house-master was old Wayne; the audio-visual had been a marionette drunkard, lurching away from a doll-sized lamp-post with random drunken steps in random drunken directions. He smiled at the jar.

'Well, what I want to do is sober him up. Watch!' Carl puffed and thought; he was a model of concentration; Rodin had only sketched the rough outlines, compared to Master Carl. Then he panted. 'Well?'

Apparently, Cornut thought, what Carl had been trying to do was to make the molecules move in straight lines. 'I don't think I see a thing,' he admitted.

'No. Neither do I. ... Well,' said Master Carl, retrieving his jar, 'even a negative answer is an answer. But I haven't given up yet. I have a few more thoughts on photographs – if Greenlease can give me a little help.' He sat down next to Cornut. 'And you?'

'You saw.'

Carl nodded seriously. 'I saw that you were still alive. Was it because you were on your own drunkard's walk?'

Cornut shook his head. He didn't mean No, he meant, How can I tell?

'And my idea about finding a wife?'

'I don't know.'

'That girl in the dining hall,' Carl said with some acuteness. 'How about her?'

'Locille? Oh, good God, Carl, how do I know about her? I – I hardly know her name. Anyway, she seems to be pretty close to Egerd.'

Carl got up and wandered to the window. 'Might as well have breakfast. The aborigines ought to be ready now.' He started at the crimson morning. 'Madam Sant'Anna has asked for a helper to get her aborigines to Valparaiso,' he said thoughtfully. 'I think I'll help her out.'

Chapter Six

Ten thousand miles away, in the early afternoon, Locille was not very close to Egerd at all. 'Sorry,' she said. 'I *would* like to. But –'

Egerd stood huffily up. 'What's the record?' he said angrily. 'Ten weeks? Good enough. I'll be around to see you again along about the first of the month.' He stalked out of the girls' dayroom.

Locille sighed, but as she did not know what to do about Egerd's jealousy, she did nothing. It was rather difficult to be a girl sometimes.

For here's Locille, a girl, pretty enough, full of a girl's problems. It is a girl's business to keep her problems to herself. It is a girl's business to look poised and lovely. And available.

It is not true that girls are made of sugar and spice. These mysterious creatures, enamelled of complexion faintly scented with distant flower-fields and musk, constricted *here* and enlarged *there* – they are animals, as men are animals, sustained by the same sludgy trickle of partly fermented organic matter; and indeed with a host of earthy problems men need never know, the oestral flow, the burgeoning cells that replenish the race. Womanhood has always been a triumph of artifice over the animal within.

And here, as we say, is Locille. Twenty years old, student, child of a retired subway engineer and his retired social-worker wife. She is young, she is nubile.

The state of her health is a ploughmare's. What can she know of mysteries?

But she knew.

On the night the Field Expedition was due to return, Locille was excused from all her evening classes. She took advantage of an hour of freedom to telephone her parents, out on the texas. She discovered as she had discovered a hundred times before that there was nothing to say between them; and returned to the kitchens of the Faculty Mess in time to take up her duties for the evening.

The occasion was the return of the Field Expedition. It promised to be a monstrous feast.

More than two hundred visiting notables would be present, as well as most of the upper faculty of the University itself. The kitchens were buzzing with activity. All six C. E.s were on duty, all busy; the culinary engineer in charge of sauces and gravies spied Locille first and drafted her to help him, but there was a struggle; the engineer whose charge was pastries knew her and wanted her too. Sauces and gravies won out, and Locille found herself emulsifying caked steer blood and powdered spices in a huge metal vat; the sonic whine of the emulsifier and the staccato hiss of the steam as she valved it expertly into the mixture drowned out the settling roar of the jet; the party had returned without her knowing it; the first clue she had was when there was a commotion at one end of the kitchens, and she turned, and there was Egerd, dourly shepherding three short, sallow persons she didn't recognize.

He saw her. 'Locille! Come on over and meet the aborigines!'

She hesitated and glanced at her C. E., who pantomimed take-ten-if-it-won't-spoil-the-gravy. Locille slipped off her gauntlets, set the automatic timers and thermostats and ducked past the kneading, baking, pressure-cooking machines of the Faculty Kitchen towards Egerd and his trophies.

'They're Japanese,' he said proudly. 'You've heard of War Two? They were abandoned on an island, and their descendants have been there ever since. Say, Locille –'

She took her eyes off the aborigines to look at Egerd. He seemed both angry and proud. 'I have to go to Valparaiso,' he said. 'There are six other aborigines who are going to South America, and Master Carl picked me to go along.'

She started to answer, but Cornut was wandering into the room, looking thoughtful.

Egerd looked thoughtfully, back at him.

'I wondered why Carl picked me for this,' he said, not bitterly but with comprehension. 'All right.' He turned to leave through another door. 'He can have his chance – for the next sixteen days,' he said.

Thoughtful Cornut was. He had never proposed marriage before. 'Hello, Locille,' he said formally.

She said, 'Hello, Master Cornut.'

He said, 'I, uh, want to ask you something.'

She said nothing. He looked around the kitchen as though he had never been in it before, which was probably so. He said, 'Would you like to – ah, would you like to meet me on Overlook Tower tomorrow?'

'Certainly, Master Cornut.'

'That's fine,' he said politely, nodding, and was halfway into the dining-room before he realized he hadn't told her when. Maybe she thought he expected her to stand there all day long! He hurried back. 'At noon?'

'All right.'

'And don't make any plans for the evening,' he commanded, hurrying away. It was embarrassing. He had never proposed marriage before, and had not succeeded in proposing now, he thought. But he was wrong. He had. He didn't know it, but Locille did.

The rest of the evening passed very rapidly for Cornut. The dinner was a great success. The aborigines were a howl. They passed among the guests, smoking their pipe of peace with everyone who cared to try it, which was everyone, and as the guests got drunker the aborigines, responding to every toast with a loud *Banzai!*, then a hoarse one, then a simper – the aborigines got drunker still.

Cornut had a ball. He caught glimpses of Locille from time to time at first, then not. He asked after her, asked the waitresses, asked the aborigines, finally found himself asking – or telling – about Locille with his arm around the flaccid shoulders of Master Wahl. He was quite drunk early, and he kept on drinking. He had moments of clarity: Master Carl listened patiently while Cornut tried to demonstrate Brownian motion in a rye-and-ginger-ale; a queer, alone moment when he realized he was staggering around the empty kitchen, calling Locille's name to the cold copper cauldrons. Somehow, God knows how, he found himself in the elevators of Math Tower, when it must have been very late, and Egerd in a cream-coloured robe was trying to help him into his room. He knew he said something to Egerd that must have been either coarse or cruel, because the boy turned away from him and did not protest when Cornut locked his door, but he did not know what. Had he mentioned Locille? When had he not! He fell sprawled on his bed, giggling. He had mentioned Locille a thousand times, he knew, and stroked the pillow beside him.

He drifted off to sleep.

He drifted off to sleep and halted, for a moment sober, for a moment terrified, knowing that he was on the verge of sleep, again alone. But he could not stop.

He could not stop because he was a molecule in a sea of soapy soup and Master Carl was hurling him into the arms of Locille.

Master Carl was hurling him away because Egerd had hurled him at Master Carl; Locille thrust him at St Cyr and St Cyr, voicelessly chuckling, hurled him clear out of the jar, and he could not stop.

He could not stop because St Cyr told him: You are a molecule, drunken molecule, you are a molecule, drunk and random, without path, you are a drunken molecule and you cannot stop.

He could not stop though the greatest voice in the world was shouting at him:

YOU CAN ONLY DIE, DRUNKEN MOLECULE, YOU CAN DIE, YOU CANNOT STOP.

He could not stop because the world was reeling, reeling, he tried to open his eyes to halt it but it would not stop.

He was a molecule.

He saw that he was a molecule and he saw he could not stop.

Then –
the molecule
– stopped.

Chapter Seven

Egerd tried pounding on the locked door for nearly five minutes and then went away. He could have stayed longer, but he didn't want to; he thought it out carefully and concluded, first, that he had done what he undertook to do – in spite of the fact that Cornut's choosing to marry Locille upset the undertaking; and second, that if he was too late he was already too late.

Nearly an hour later Cornut woke up.

He was alive, he noticed with interest.

It had been a most peculiar dream. It did not seem like a dream. His afternoon lecture, with Pogo Possum drawling hickory-bark rules for factoring large integers, was much more fantasy in his mind than the dream-scene of himself contemplating himself, staggering drunk and with a bottle in his hand, trapped in the ceaseless Brownian zigzag. He knew that the only way a molecule could stop was to die, but curiously he had not died.

He got up, dressed and went out.

He was remarkably hung over, but it was much, much better outside. It was bright morning and, he remembered very clearly, he had an engagement with Locille for that morning.

He was on tape for the A.M. lecture; it gave him the morning off. He walked about the campus aimlessly, past the green steel and glass of the Stadium, past the broad lawns of the lower campus to the Bridge. The Med School lay huddled under the Bridge itself. He liked the Bridge, liked its sweep across the Bay, liked the way it condescended to drop one pylon to the island where the University had been built. He very much liked that pylon; that was Overlook Tower.

On impulse, thinking that this was a good time to be quite sober, he stopped at the Clinic to get a refill on his wake-up pills. The clinic was not manned at that hour, except for emergencies, but as Cornut was a returnee he was admitted to the automatic diagnosis machines. It was very much the same as the experience of three nights before, except that there was no human doctor at all. A mechanical finger inserted a hair-thin tendril into his arm and tasted his blood, compared it with the recent chromatograph, and whirred thoughtfully while it considered if there had been changes. In a moment the *Solution* light winked pink, there was a click and clatter, and in a hopper by his hand there dropped a plastic box of his pills.

He took one. Ah, fine! They were working. It was a strange and rewarding sensation. Whatever the pills contained, they fought fatigue at first encounter. He could trace the course of that first pill clear down his throat and into his abdomen. The path tingled with well-being. He felt pretty good. No, he felt *very* good. He walked out into the fresh air again, humming to himself.

It was a long climb up the pylon to Overlook Landing, but he did it on foot, feeling comfortable all the way. He popped another pill into his mouth and waited in patient good humour for Locille.

She came promptly from her class.

From the base of the pylon she glanced up at the Overlook Landing, nearly two hundred feet over her head. If Cornut was there she couldn't see him. She rode up on the outside escalators, twining round the huge hexagonal tower, for the sake of the air and the view. It *was* a lovely view – the clean white rectahedron of the biologicals factory, the dome-shaped Clinic under the spreading feet of the pylon itself, the bright University buildings, the green of the lawns, the two dissimilar blues of water and sky. Lovely. . . .

But she was nervous. She stepped off the escalator, turned around the bulk of the pylon and bowed. 'Master Cornut,' she said.

The wind caught at her blouse and hair. Cornut stood dreaming over the rail, his own short hair blown carelessly around his forehead. He turned idly and smiled with sleepy eyes. 'Ah,' he said. 'Locille.' He nodded as though she had answered – she had not. 'Locille,' he said, 'I need a wife. You will do.'

'Thank you, Master Cornut.'

He waved a gentle hand. 'You aren't engaged, I understand?'

'No.' Unless you counted Egerd – but *she* didn't count Egerd.

'Not pregnant, I presume?'

'No. I have never been pregnant.'

'Oh, no matter, no matter,' he said hastily. 'I don't mind that. It isn't any sort of physical problem, I suppose?'

'No.' She didn't meet his eye this time, though. For there *was* a sort of physical problem, in a way. There couldn't have been a pregnancy without a man. She had avoided that.

She stood waiting for him to say something else, but he was a long time in getting around to it. Out of the corner of her eye she noted that he was taking pills out of that little box as though they were candy. She wondered if he knew he was taking them. She remembered the knife-edge at his throat in class; she remembered the stories Egerd had told. Silly business; why would anyone try to kill himself?

He collected himself and cleared his throat, taking another pill. 'Let me see,' he mused. 'No engagements on record, no physical bars, no consanguinity, of course – I'm an only child, you see. Well, I think that's everything, Locille. Shall we say tonight, after late class?' He looked suddenly concerned. 'Oh, that is – you have no objection, do you?'

'I have no objection.'

'Good.' He nodded, but his face remained clouded. 'Locille,' he began, 'perhaps you've heard stories about me. I – I have had a number of accidents lately. And one reason why I wish to take a wife is to guard against any more accidents. Do you understand?'

'I understand that, Master Cornut.'

'Very good. Very good.' He took another pill out of the box, hesitated, glanced at it.

His eyes widened.

Not understanding, Locille stood motionless; she didn't know that a sudden realization had come to Master Cornut.

It was the last pill in the box. But there had been twenty at least! Twenty, not more than three-quarters of an hour before – twenty!

He cried hoarsely, 'Another accident!'

It was as if the realization released the storm of the pills. Cornut's pulse began to pound. His head throbbed in a new and faster tempo. The world spun scarlet around him. A rush of bile clogged his throat.

'Master Cornut!'

But it was already too late for the girl to cry out – he

67

knew; he had acted. He hurled the box out into space, stared at her, crimson, then without ceremony leaped to the rail.

Locille screamed.

She was after him, clutching at him, but impatiently he shrugged her off, and then she saw that he was not climbing to hurl himself to death; he had his finger down his throat; without romance or manners, Master Cornut was getting the poison out of him quickly, efficiently –

And all by himself.

Locille stood by silently, waiting.

After a few minutes his shoulders stopped heaving, but he leaned on the rail, staring, for minutes after that. When he turned his face was the racked face of a damned soul.

'I'm sorry. Thanks.'

Locille said softly, 'But I didn't do anything.'

'Of course you did. You woke me up –'

She shook her head. 'You did it by yourself, you know. You did.'

He looked at her with irritation, then with doubt. And then at last, he looked at her with the beginning of hope.

Chapter Eight

The ceremony was very simple. Master Carl officiated. There was a friendly meal, and then they were left alone, Locille and Cornut, by the grace of the magisterial power inherent in house-masters, man and wife.

They went to his room.

'You'd better rest,' said Locille.

'All right.' He sprawled on the bed to watch her. He was very much aware of her, now studying, now doing womanlike tasks about his room – no. *Their* room. She was as inconspicuous as a flesh-and-blood person could be, moving quickly when she moved. But she might have been neon-lit and blaring with sirens for the way she kept distracting him.

He stood up and dressed himself, not looking at her. She said questioningly: 'It's time for sleep, isn't it?'

He fumbled. 'Is it?' But the clock said yes; it was; he had slept the day through. 'All right,' he said, as though it were some trivial thing and not world-shaking at all. 'Yes, it's time for – sleep. But I think I will take a walk around the campus, Locille. I need it.'

'Certainly.' She nodded and waited, polite and calm.

'Perhaps I shall be back before you are asleep,' he went on. 'Perhaps not. Perhaps I –' He was rambling. He nodded, cleared his throat, picked up his cloak and left.

No one was in the corridor outside, no one in sight in the hall.

There was a thin electronic *peep* from the robot night-proctors, but that was all right. Master Cornut was no undergraduate, to wriggle under the sweep of the scanning beams on his belly. It was his privilege to come and go as he chose.

He chose to go.

He walked out on to the campus, quiet under a yellow moon, the bridge overhead ghostly silver. There was no *reason* why he should be so emotionally on edge. Locille was only a student.

The fact remained, he was on edge.

But why should he be? Student marriage was good for the students, good for the masters; custom sanctioned it; and Master Carl, from the majesty of his housemaster's post, had suggested it in the first place.

Queerly, he kept thinking of Egerd.

There had been a look on young Egerd's face, and maybe it was that which bothered him. Master Cornut was not so many years past his sheepskin that he could quite dismiss the possible emotions of an undergraduate. Custom, privilege and law to one side, the fact remained that a student quite often did feel jealous of a master's prerogatives. While a student, Cornut himself had contracted no liaisons to be interfered with. But other students had. And there was no doubt that, in Egerd's immature, undergraduate way, he might well be jealous.

But what did that matter? His jealousy could harm only himself. No serf, raging inwardly against his lord's *jus primae noctis*, was less able to make his anger felt than Egerd. But somehow Cornut was feeling it.

He felt almost guilty.

He was no logician, his field was Mathematics. But this whole concept of *right*, he thought as he paced along the riverbank, needed some study. What the world sanctioned was clear: The rights of the higher displaced the rights of the lower, as an atom of fluorine will drive oxygen out of a compound. But *should* it be that way?

It *was* that way – if that was an answer.

And all of class, all of privilege, all of law, seemed to be working to produce one single commodity – a product which, of all the world's goods, is unique in that it has never been in short supply, never quite satisfied its demand and never failed to find a market: Babies. Wherever you looked, babies. In the crèches in the women's dorms, in the playrooms attached to the rooms of the masters – babies. It was almost as though it had been planned that way; custom and law determined the fact that as many adult humans as possible spend as much of their time as possible in performing the acts that made babies arrive. Why? What was the drive that produced so many *babies*?

It wasn't a matter of sex alone – it was *babies*. Sex was perfectly possible and joyous under conditions that made the occurrence of *babies* utterly impossible; science had arranged that decades, even centuries, before. But contraception was – well, *wrong*. And so, all over the world, this uncomplicated and unaided practice of baby-making added a clear two per cent to the world's population every time the earth sailed around the sun.

Two per cent per year!

There were now something over twelve billion persons alive. Next year's census would show four hundred million more than that.

And why?

What made babies so popular?

Crazy as it was, the conclusion forced itself on Master Cornut: It was *planned* that way.

By whom, he wondered, settling down to a long night's thoughtful ramble and pursuing of the line of thought to its last extreme –

But not tonight; because he looked up and there was his own dorm. His feet had known more clearly than he the ultimate answer to the question: *Babies?*

He was back at the entrance of Math Tower where the girl, Locille, was waiting.

The thing was, the bed.

She had had a bed of her own moved into the room, for that was the way it was done; but of course there was his bed already there, much larger, so that –

Well, which bed would she be in?

He took a deep breath, nodded blindly to the unseeing electronic night proctor, and opened the door of his room.

A riotous alarm bell shattered the stillness.

Master Cornut stood staring, stupidly, while the flesh-and-blood undergraduate charged with supervising the corridors came peering worriedly around the corner, drawn by the sound; and the bell continued to ring. Then he realized it was connected with the door; it was his automatic alarm bell, rigged by himself. But he had not connected it this night, he knew.

He stepped in quickly, threw a scowl back at the undergraduate, and closed the door. The ringing stopped.

Locille was rising from the bed – *his* bed.

Her hair was soft about her head and her eyes were downcast but bright. She had not been asleep. She said, 'You must be tired. Would you like me to fetch you something to eat?'

He said in a tremblingly stern voice: 'Locille, why did you bug the door?'

She looked at him. 'Why, to wake me up when you came in. The bell was there; I only had to turn it on.'

'And why?'

'Why,' she said, 'I wanted to.' And she yawned, rather prettily; and excused herself with a smile; and turned to straighten the covers on the bed.

Cornut, watching her from behind as he had never watched her from the front, made note of two incredible facts.

The first was that this girl, Locille, was beautiful. She was wearing very little, only a sleeping skirt and a sleeping yoke, and there was no doubt of her figure; and she was wearing no make-up that the eye could see, and there was no doubt about her face. Beautiful. Amazing, Cornut told himself, conscious of commotions inside himself, amazing, but I want this girl very much.

And that led him to the other fact, which was more incredible still.

Cornut had picked her out as a shopper might select one roast over another. Cornut had told her what to do; Cornut had, as far as he possibly could, arranged to destroy, with method and plan, everything of eagerness and spontaneous joy there might have been. It was his peculiar fortune that he had failed.

He looked at her and knew what had never entered into his calculations. It had never occurred to him that she might be eager for *him*.

Rap, tap.

The girl shook him awake – fully awake. 'What do you want?' Cornut cried crossly at the door. Beside him, Locille made a face, a sweet, a mock-arrogant face, that was a tender caricature of his own; so that by the time the morning proctor opened the door a crack and peered around it, Cornut was smiling at him. Wonders never-ceasing, thought the proctor, and said timidly, 'Master Cornut, it is eight o'clock.'

Cornut drew the covers over Locille's bare shoulder. 'Go away,' he said.

The door closed, and one of Locille's pink slippers slapped lightly against it. She raised the other to toss after the first. Cornut caught her arm, laughing very softly; and she turned to him, not quite laughing, and kissed him, and sprang away.

'And *stay* awake,' she warned. 'I have to go to class.'

Cornut leaned back against the pillowcase.

Why, it was a pleasant morning, he thought, and maybe in a way a pleasant world! It was perfectly amazing what hues and brightnesses there were in the world, that he had either never suspected or long forgot. He watched the girl, miraculously a part of his life, a segment joined on without a trace or seam where he had never suspected a segment was missing. She moved lightly around the room, and she looked at him from time to time; and if she wasn't asmile like a grinning ape it was because there wasn't any need for smiles just then, of course.

Cornut was a well satisfied man that morning.

Quick-quick, she was dressed; much too quickly. 'You,' said Cornut, 'are in much too much of a hurry to be gone from here.'

Locille came and sat on the edge of the bed. Even in the uniform she was beautiful now. That was another amazing thing. It was like knowing that a chalice was purest gold under the enamel; the colours were the same, the design was the same; but suddenly what had been a factory product was become a work of art, simply through knowing what graces lay underneath. She said,

'That is because I am in a hurry to return.' She looked at him again and said questioningly, 'You won't go back to sleep?'

'Of course not.' She was frowning slightly, he saw with fondness; reminding him of the reason he had sought a companion in the first place; *that* old reason.

'All right.' She kissed him, rose, found her carry-all where she had left it on a chair, and her books. She caroled softly to herself. 'Strike the Twos and strike the Threes, the Sieve of Eratosthenes. When the multiples – Cornut, you're *sure* you won't go back to sleep?'

'Sure.'

She nodded, hesitating with one hand on the door. She said doubtfully, 'Maybe you'd better take a wake-up pill. Will you?'

'I will,' he said, rejoicing in being nagged.

'And you'd better start dressing yourself in a few minutes. It's only half an hour until your first class – '

'I know.'

'All right.' She blew him a kiss, and a smile; and she was gone.

And the room was very empty. But not as empty as it had been all the days and nights before.

Cornut dutifully got up, found himself the pillbox with the red and green sleeping regulators, took one and returned to bed; he had never felt better in his life.

He lay back against the pillow, utterly relaxed and at peace. He had bought himself an alarm clock and it turned out to be a wife. He smiled at the low cream-coloured ceiling, and stretched and yawned. What a perfectly fine bargain! What a super-perfect alarm clock!

And that reminded him; and he glanced at his watch; but he'd taken it off and the wall clock was out of his angle of vision. Well, no matter; the wake-up pill would keep him from going back to sleep again. It was common knowledge that the wake-up pill made time run short. It felt as though he had been lying here half an hour; well, it couldn't be more than five minutes; that was how they worked.

Still. . . .

He fumbled in the little divided box. Fortunate that they were handy; another pill would make doubly sure.

He swallowed it, leaned back again and yawned. There was something about the pillow, he thought. . . .

He turned his head, sniffed, breathed deeply. Yes. There was Locille about the pillow; that was what it was. Locille, who left a fragrance behind her. Beautiful fragrance of Locille, beautiful name. Beautiful girl. He caught himself yawning again –

Yawning?

Yawning!

He blinked the eyes that were much too heavy, and tried to turn the very weary head. Yawning! But after two wake-up pills – or was it three, or six?

History was repeating!

Red pills for wake-up, green for sleep. The green pills, he sobbed in his thoughts, he'd been taking the *green* ones!

He was caught.

Oh, Lord, he whimpered soundlessly – oh, Lord, why this time? Why did you wait to catch me until I *cared*?

Chapter Nine

The assistant audio engineer, staring bemused through the glass at the filling studio, was humming to himself. It irritated Master Carl. He could not help fitting words to the tune:

> Strike the Twos and strike the Threes:
> The Sieve of Eratosthenes!
> When the multiples sublime,
> The numbers that are left, are prime.

It did not alleviate his annoyance that the song was one of his own. Classic Prime-Number Exposition was not the subject of the morning's class; it was Set Theory; he snapped, 'Be still, man! Don't you like your work here?' The assistant audio engineer paled. He had been brought up on a texas and never forgot that he might some day have to go back to one.

It was not really true that the humming distracted him. At Master Carl's age, you either know what you are doing or you don't, and he knew. He went out at the precise moment his theme began and spoke the words he always spoke, while his mind was on Cornut, on the Wolgren anomaly, on his private investigation of the paranormal, on – especially on – the responses and behaviour of each individual undergraduate in his in-studio audience. He noted every yawn of a drowsy nucleonics major in the far corner; he observed with particular care the furtive passage of notes from the boy, Egerd, to his protégé's new wife, Locille. He did not intend to do anything about it. He was grateful to Locille. As a good watchdog, she might very well save the life of the only man on the faculty Carl considered to have any chance of ever replacing himself.

In five minutes he had concluded the live portion of his lecture and, indulging his own harmless desires, left the studio. Taped figures danced on the screen behind him, singing *The Ballad of Sets.*

> Let 'S' be a number set, them progress:
> If, of any two numbers (a and b) in S,
> Their sum is also in the set,
> The set is *closed!* And so we get
> A *reproductive set* with this definition:
> 'The number set S is closed by addition!'

He put the class out of his mind and eagerly drew a sheaf of photographic prints out of his briefcase. He had slept only restlessly the night before and had risen early to work at his newest hobby. He had had many. He needed many. Carl was in no way dissatisfied, could not have conceived a world in which he would not have been a mathematician, but it wasn't all pleasure to be a towering elder statesman in a young man's game. It was a queer fact of mathematics that nearly every great mathematician had done his best work before he was thirty. And most of them, like Carl, had turned to other curiosities in their later years.

Someone opened the door and the choral voices from the studio surged in on him:

> If number set M is closed by subtraction,
> A *modul* is the term for this transaction!

Master Carl turned, frowning like ice. Egerd! He demanded terribly, 'What is a number set closed by multiplication?'

Egerd quailed but said, 'It's a ray, Master Carl. It's in the fourth canto. Sir, I want to – '

'Closed to addition and subtraction as well?'

'A ring, sir. Can I speak to you a moment?'

Carl grunted.

'I did study the lesson, Master Carl. As you can see.'

He would have said more, but Carl had not finished being stern. 'There is no excuse, Egerd, for leaving a class without permission. You must know that. It may seem to you that you are able to grasp set theory by studying from books, no doubt. You are wrong. A mathematician must know these simple classical facts and definition as well as he knows that February has twenty-eight days, and in the same way. By mnemonics! I assure you that you will never become a first-rate mathematician by cutting classes.'

'Yes, sir. That's it. I want to transfer out. As soon as I get back from South America, if it's all right with you, sir.'

Master Carl was purely horrified.

This was not a case for discipline, he saw at once. Carl did not consider that the separation of Egerd from mathematics would be a loss to mathematics. It was compassion for the boy himself that gave him concern. 'Well. What is it you want to transfer to?'

'Med School, sir. I've made up my mind.' He added, 'You can understand why, Master Carl. I don't have much talent for this stuff.'

Carl didn't understand; he would never understand. He had, however, some long time before that made up his mind that there were things about his students that didn't need much understanding. His students had many facets; only one concerned him. They were like those paper patterns the soft-headed undergraduates in Topology played with, hexihexiflexagons, constructions that turned up new sides in bewildering variety each time they were flexed. He said mournfully, 'All right. I'll sign your release.' He scowled when he saw that Egerd already had it filled out and ready for him; the boy was *too* eager.

The door opened again.

Master Carl halted with the pen in his hand. 'Now what?' He recognized the man – vaguely – it was that hanger-on of the Department of Liberal Arts. The name escaped him, but he was a sex-writer. He was also agitated.

The man said, 'Excuse me. I'm sorry. Name's Farley. I'm Master Cornut's – '

'You're a sex-writer. I have no objection to that. I do object to having my privacy disturbed.' Although that was not quite true either. Master Carl was prude enough (perhaps because he was woman-shy enough) to feel that the private affairs of men and women should not be inspired by scripts provided by sex-writers or, as they were once called, marriage counsellors. *He* would never have employed one, and he was irked with Cornut.

As it turned out, neither would Cornut. 'I was a wedding present,' Farley explained, 'and so I went to see Cornut this morning with a rough thirty-day draft. I don't use standard forms; I believe in personalized counselling. So I thought I'd better interview the male subject right away because, as you know – '

Egerd interrupted desperately, 'Master Carl. Please sign my transfer.'

The expression in his eyes said more than his words. The flexagon turned up another side, and this time Carl was able to read its design. He nodded and wrote his name. It was entirely clear that Egerd's reasons for transferring away from Locille and Master Cornut had nothing much to do with his talent for mathematics.

But the sex-writer would not be stopped. 'Then where is the female subject, Master Carl?' he demanded. 'They said she would be here. . . .'

'Locille? Of course.' A terrible thought entered Carl's mind. 'You mean that something happened – *again*? When you went to see Cornut he was – '

'Out cold, yes. Almost dead. He's having his stomach pumped now, though; they think he'll be all right.'

When they reached Cornut's room, the medic was scanning a spectrum elaborated for him by a portable diagnosticon. Cornut himself was unconscious. The medic reassured them. 'Close, but he missed this time. What was it, his fifteenth? And the record is – '

Carl interrupted frostily. 'Can you wake him up? Good. Then do.'

The medic shrugged and fished for a hypodermic. He slipped the piston of the needle into the barrel; the faint spray appeared, hovering over Cornut's unbroken skin. The tiny droplets found their way through dermis and epidermis and subcutaneous fat and, in a moment, Cornut sat up.

He said clearly, 'I had the most ridiculous dream.'

And then he saw Locille; and his face was alight. That at least was no dream. Master Carl had little tact, but he had enough to take the medic and leave the two of them there.

The experience of having one's stomach pumped is not attractive. This was Cornut's third time, but he had not come to like it; he tasted bile and foulness, his oesophagus had been painfully scraped; the sleeping pills had left him with a headache.

'I'm sorry,' he said.

Locille brought him a glass and one of the capsules the medic had left. He swallowed it and began to chuckle. 'Lucky Wahl,' he said. 'You know, if I'd been awake when that fellow came in I'd have gone over and punched Wahl in the head; it was his idea; he got half of Anthropology to chip in to buy us Farley's services for a year. As it is. . . . I guess Wahl saved my life.' He got up and began to wander around. In spite of the taste and the head, he was feeling rather cheerful, in an un-analysed way. Even the dream, though queer, had not been unpleasant. Master Carl had been in it, and so had St Cyr and the woman from South America; but so had Locille.

He paused by his desk. 'What's this?' It was a neat sheaf of papers clipped in a folder on which was printed: *S. R. Farley, Consultant.* That was all. Just *Consultant*. He opened it and found the first page a cleanly typed set of what seemed to be equations. The symbols ♂ and ♀ occurred frequently, along with strokes, daggers and congruencies which he vaguely remembered from an undergraduate course in symbolic logic. 'That's almost a Boolean notation,' he said interestedly. 'I wonder – Say, look at this, Locille. Line three. If you substitute these three terms from the expansion in line four, and –'

He stopped. She was blushing. But he hadn't noticed; he was suddenly scowling at his desk. 'My Wolgren! Where is it?'

'If you mean the report on distributive anomalies you were preparing for Master Carl, he took it as he went out.'

'But it isn't finished!'

'But he didn't want you working on it. Or anything.

He wants you to take the day off – get off the campus – and he wants me to stay with you.'

'Huh.' He stared glumly at the window. 'Hum.' He made tasting motions with his lips and tongue and made a face. 'Well. All right. Where is there to go, off campus? Do you have any ideas?'

Locille looked a little worried. 'As a matter of fact,' she said diffidently, 'I do. . . .'

At sundown they boarded the one-a-day ferry to the texas; there was traffic enough from the city to the texas, and even from the University to the city; but between the texas and the University there was almost none. They leaned against the rail as the ferry rose, looking down at the University's island, the city and the bay. The almost silent blades overhead chopped the scarlet sunset sky into dots and dashes; all they could hear inside the domed deck of the ferry was a bass flutter of blades and a more-than-soprano hiss of the blade-tip jets.

Locille said abruptly, 'I didn't tell you about Roger. My brother,' she said swiftly.

Cornut stopped an emotion before it had quite got started. 'What about him?' he asked, relieved.

She said flatly, 'He isn't University calibre. He might have been, but – When Roger was about five years old – he was swimming off the texas – there was another boy in the water, and he dived. They collided. The other boy drowned.' She paused, turning to look at him. 'Roger fractured his skull. Ever since then, he's been – well, his intelligence never developed much past that point.'

Cornut received the information, frowning.

It was not that he minded a stupid brother-in-law; it was only that he had never thought of there being any brother-in-law at all. It had never occurred to Cornut that marriage involved more than two people.

'He isn't insane,' Locille said worriedly, 'just not intelligent.'

Cornut hardly heard her. He was busy trying to cope with the thought that there was more here than watchdog or love; there was something here that he had never counted on. It took twenty minutes to fly the rest of the way to the texas, and it took all of that time for Cornut to puzzle out the fact that he had taken on more than a convenience or a pleasure, he had assumed a sort of obligation as well.

The texas stood in ninety feet of water, just over the horizon from Sandy Hook. It was fifteen acres of steel decks, twelve levels high, the lowest of the levels forty feet above mean high water. It was not the fault of the designers of the texas that 'mean high water' was an abstraction, the average distance between trough and peak of the great swells of the ocean. The texas crouched on hundreds of metal legs that sank into the ooze to the bedrock beneath, and it was a target. In storms the whitecaps slapped demandingly at its underbelly. If there was lightning, it was sure to strike at the radar beacon on its tower.

Time was when those radars had been the reason for the existence of texas towers. That time was past; satellite eyes and ionosphere-scatter search methods had ended their importance. But the world had found other uses for them. They guided the whale-backed submersibles of the world's cargo fleets as they surfaced over the continental shelf to find harbour; they served as mother 'ships' for the ranging fishery fleets in shallow seas. They provided living room for some tens of millions on the

American seaboard alone. They provided work space for nuisance industries – the ones that smelled, or were loud, or were dangerous.

Power was free, nearly, on a texas. Each hollow leg was slotted in its lower stretch. The waves that came crashing by compressed the air in the columns, valved through a one-way exhaust into a pressure tank; pneumatic turbines whirred at the release vents of the tanks, and the texas' lights and industries drew current from those turbines. In 'good' weather – when the waves roared and pounded – there was power to smelt aluminium; the ore boats that unloaded the raw materials carried away the slag, dumping it within sight of the texas itself in the inexhaustible disposal pit of the ocean. When weather was 'bad' – when the Atlantic was glassy smooth – aluminium making stopped for a while. But weather was never really 'bad' for long.

Locille's parents lived with her brother, in a three-room apartment in the residential area of the texas. It was leeward of the fisheries, across the texas from the aluminium refinery, six levels above the generators. Cornut thought it horrible. It smelled and it was noisy.

Locille had brought presents. A sash for her father, something cosmetic for her mother and, Cornut saw with astonishment, one of the flags the aborigines had brought with them as a gift for her brother Roger. It had not occurred to Cornut that there should be gifts, much less gifts as expensive as any aboriginal artifact; the things were in great demand as conversation pieces. But he was grateful. The flag was a conversation piece here, too, and he needed one. Locille's mother brought out coffee and cake, and Cornut entertained them with his trip to the South Seas.

He did not, however, mention his blackout by the side of the road; and he could not keep his eyes off Roger.

Locille's brother was a huge young man, taller than Cornut, with a pleasant expression and dull eyes. He was not offered coffee and refused cake; he sat there, watching Cornut, fingering the worn fabric of his gift, even smelling it, rubbing it against his face. Cornut found him disconcerting. Barring the aborigines and a handful of clinical cases under study, there was not one human being on the campus with an I.Q. under a hundred and forty, and Cornut had no experience of the simple-minded. The boy could talk – but mostly did not – and though he seemed to understand what Cornut was saying, he never changed expression.

The fact of the matter was that Roger didn't much care what Cornut was saying. His whole attention was taken up with his gift. As soon as he thought it was proper to do so, he excused himself and carried it to his room.

Roger was aware that it was very old and came from very far away; but that could have been something of last week's, from the city just below the horizon; he had little memory. What Roger thought principally about the flag was that it was a pretty colour.

He tacked it with magnetic grips to the wall of his room, stood back thoughtfully, removed the grips and replaced it closer to his bed. He stood there looking at it, because somehow it satisfied him to stand and look at it.

It was bright moonlight outside, but there was a fair wind sweeping across the long reach from Portugal. The waves were high; and the pneumatic hammer-hammer and the rattle-slam of the valves opening and closing pounded through the texas, one noise reinforcing the other. It made it hard for anyone to talk in the other room. (Cornut was growing more and more uneasy.) But it didn't bother Roger. Since the day his own crushed skull had minced a corner of his brain, nothing had really *bothered* Roger.

But he liked the flag. After ten minutes of staring at it, he took off the magnets that held it, folded it and put it under his pillow. Smiling with pleasure, he went back into the other room to say good-night to his sister's new husband.

Chapter Ten

Master Carl lighted a do-not-disturb sign on his door and opened the folding screen that hid his little darkroom from the casual eyes of the student housekeepers. He was not ashamed of the hobby that made him operate a darkroom; it was simply none of their business. Carl was not ashamed of anything he did. His room attested to that; it bore the marks of all his interests.

Three boards held chess problems half worked out and forgotten, the pieces lifted, dusted and replaced by a dozen generations of student maids. On the cream-and-lilac walls were framed prints of Minoan scenes and inscriptions, the ten-year-old relics of his statistical examination into the grammar of Linear B. A carton that had once contained two dozen packs of Rhine cards (and still contained five unopened packs) showed the two years he had spent in demonstrating to his own satisfaction, once for all, that telepathy was not possible.

The proof rested on an analogy, but Master Carl had satisfied himself that the analogy was valid. If, he supposed, telepathic communication could be subsumed under the general equations of Unified Field Law, it had to fall into one of the two possible categories therein. It could be tunable, like the electromagnetic spectrum; or it could be purely quantitative, like the kinetogravitic realms. He eliminated the second possibility at once: it implied that every thought would be received by every person within range, and observation denied that on the face of it.

Telepathy, then, if it existed at all, had to be tunable. Carl then applied his analogy. Crystals identical in structure resonate at the same frequency. Humans identical in structure do exist: they are called identical twins. For two years Master Carl had spent most of his free time locating, persuading and testing pairs of identical twins. It took two years, and no more, because that was how long it took him to find three hundred and twenty-six pairs; and three hundred and twenty-six was the number the chi-square law gave as the minimum universe in which a statistical sampling could be regarded as conclusive. When the three hundred and twenty-sixth twin had failed to secure significantly more than chance correlation with the card symbols viewed by his sibling, Carl had closed out the experiment at once.

When the two-year job was ended Carl was not angry, but he was also not hopeful. It did not occur to him to go on to a three hundred and twenty-seventh set. He did, however, permit himself to turn at once to investigating other aspects of what had once been called psionics.

Precognition he eliminated on logical grounds; clairvoyance he pondered over for several months before deciding that, like the conjecture that flying saucers were of extra-terrestrial origin, it offered too few opportunities for experimental verification to be an attractive study. Hexing he ruled out as necessarily involving either telepathy or clairvoyance. It was not the cases in which the sufferer knew he was hexed that offered a problem; simple suggestion could account for most of those; a man who saw the wax doll with the pins in it, or was told by the ju-ju man that his toenails were being roasted, might very easily sicken and die out of fear. But if the victim did not learn of his hex through physical means, he could learn only by either telepathy or clairvoyance; and Carl had eliminated them.

The traditional list of paranormal powers included only two other phenomena: fire-sending and telekinesis.

Carl elected to consider the first as only a subdivision of the second. Speeding the Brownian Movement of molecules (i.e., heating them) to the point of flame was surely no different in kind than gross manipulation of groups of molecules (i.e., moving material objects).

His first attempts at telekinesis involved a weary time of attempting to shift bits of matter, papers first, then balanced pins, hanging threads, finally grains of dust on a microbalance. There was no result. Co-opting some help from Classical Physics, Carl then began a series of tests involving photographic film. It was, the drafted physicists assured him, the medium in which the least physical force produced the greatest measurable effect. A photon, a free electron, almost any particle containing energy could shift the unstable molecules in the film emulsion.

Carl worked with higher and higher speed emulsions, learning tricks to make the film still more sensitive – special developers, close temperature control, pre-exposing the film to 'soak up' part of the energy necessary to produce an image. With each new batch of film he then sat for hours, attempting to paint circles, crosses and stars on the emulsions with his mind, visualizing the molecules and willing the change-over. He scissored out stencils and held them over the wrapped filmpacks, considering it possible that the psionic 'radiation' might show only as a point source. He had one temporary, and illusive, success: a plate of particularly trigger-happy film, wrapped under his pillow all one night, developed the next morning into a ghostly, wavering 'X'. Master Florian of Photo-chemistry disillusioned him. Carl had only succeeded in so sensitizing the film that it reacted to the tiny infra-red produced by his own body heat.

Master Carl's project for this night involved pre-exposing a specially manufactured batch of X-ray film, by means of contact with a sheet of luminescent paper; the faint gamma radiation from the paper needed hours to affect the emulsion, but those hours had to be accurately timed.

To fill the space of those hours, Master Carl had another pleasant task. He sent a student courier to his office for the unfinished draft he had abstracted from Cornut's room. It was headed:

A Reconciliation
Of Certain Apparent Anomalies
In Wolgren's Distributive Law

Carl drew a stiff-backed chair up to his desk and began to read, enjoying himself very much.

Wolgren's Law, which had to do with the distribution of non-uniform elements in random populations, was purely a mathematician's rule. It did not deal with material objects; it did not even deal with numerical quantities as such. Yet Wolgren's Law had found applications in every sort of sampling technique known to man, from setting parameters for rejecting inferior batches of canned sardines to predicting election results. It was a general law, but the specific rules that could be drawn from it had proved themselves in nearly every practical test.

In every test but one. One of Carl's graduate students had attempted to reconcile the Wolgren rule with census data for his doctoral thesis – queerly, the subject seemed never to have been covered. The boy had failed. He had found another subject, got his degree and was now happily designing communications systems for the TV syndicates, but in failing he had produced a problem worth the attention of a first-rate mathematician; and Carl had offered it to Cornut.

Cornut had worked on it, in his own after-hours time, for six months. Incomplete as it was, the report gave Master Carl three hours of intensive enjoyment. Trust Cornut to do a beautiful job! Carl followed every step, mumbling to himself; cocking an eyebrow at the use of chi-squared until it was proved by a daring extension of Gibb's phase-analysis rule. It was the mathematical statement that concerned him, not the subject of census figures themselves. It was only when he had finished the report and sat back, glowing, that he wondered why Cornut had thought it was not finished. But it was! Every equation checked! The constants were standard and correct, the variables were pinned down and identified with page after page of expansions.

'Very queer', said Carl to himself, staring vacantly at the bench where his X-ray film was quietly soaking up electrons. 'I wonder – '

He shrugged, and attempted to dismiss the problem. It would not be dismissed. He thought for a moment of calling in Cornut, but stopped himself; the boy would not be back from his visit to Locille's family, and even if he were it was no longer feasible to burst in on him.

Dissatisfied, Master Carl read again the last page of the report. The math was correct; this time he allowed the sense of it to penetrate: 'Of n births, the attained age of the oldest member of the population shall equal n times a constant e-log q.' Well? Why not?

Carl was irritated. He glanced at his clock. It was

only ten. Frowning, he buttoned his jacket and went out, leaving lights on, door open, report open on the desk . . . and the X-ray film still firmly taped to its gamma-emitting paper.

No one answered his knock on Cornut's door, so Carl, after a moment's thought, pushed it open. The room was empty; they had not returned from the texas.

Carl grumbled at the night proctor and dropped in the elevator to the campus. He thought a stroll might help. It was chilly, but he scarcely noticed. The q quantity, was there something wrong with that? But its expansions were all in order. He recalled, as clearly as though they were imprinted on the wall of the Administration Building ahead of him, the equations defining q; he even remembered what quantities those equations involved. Public health, warfare, food supply, a trickily derived value for the state of the public mind . . . they had all been in the accompanying tabulations.

'Good night, Carl-san.'

He stopped, blinking through the woven iron fence. He had reached the small encampment where the aborigines were housed; the captain, whatever his name was, had greeted him. 'I thought you people were off – ah, lecturing,' he finished lamely. 'On exhibition,' he had been about to say.

'Tomorrow, Carl-san,' said the waffle-faced man, offering Carl a long, feathered pipe. That had been in the briefing; it was a peace pipe, a quaint and for some reason, to the anthropologist a surprising, custom of the islanders. Carl shook his head. The man – Carl remembered his name; it was Masatura-san – said apologetically, 'You softspeak hard, sir. I smell you coming long way yesterday.'

'Really,' said Carl, not hearing a word. He was thinking about e-log and the validity of applying it; but that was all right too.

'Softspeak brownie not smell good,' the man explained seriously.

'No, of course not.' Carl was wondering about the values for a, the age factor in the final equation.

Tai-i Masatura-san said, growing agitated, 'Cornut-san smell bad also, St Cyr-san speak. Carl-san! Not speak brownie!'

Master Carl glanced at him. 'Certainly,' he said. 'Good night.' After him the tai-i called beseechingly, but Carl still did not hear; he had realized what it was that was unfinished about Cornut's report. The numerical values had been given for every quantity but one. It was still early; he did not intend to sleep until he had that one remaining value ...

Cornut, with his arm around Locille, yawned into the face of the red moon that hung over the horizon. It was growing very late.

They had to take the ferry to the city and wait to transfer; the only direct popper from the texas to the city was in mid-morning, and Locille's family had no place to put them up. Nor, if they had, would Cornut have stayed. He needed time to become accustomed to domesticity; it was too many things at once; bad enough that he should have to interrupt his routine to accommodate Locille's presence in his room.

But it was, on the whole, worth while.

The University was under them now, the cables of the Bridge lacing the red moon, the lights from the Administration Building bright in the dark mass of towers.

It was odd that the Administration Building should be lighted.

Drowsily Cornut looked, out of the corner of his eye, at the neat, sleepy head of his wife. He did not know if he liked her better or worse as a member of a family. The parents – dull. Amiable, he supposed, but he was used to brilliance. And her brother was an unfortunate accident, of course, but he had been so enchanted with the rag Locille had brought him, like a child, like an animal. Cornut was not quite pleased to be related to him. Of course, you couldn't choose your relatives. His own children, for example, might be quite disappointing. . . .

His own children! The thought had come quite naturally; but he had never had that particular thought before. Involuntarily he shivered, and looked again at Locille.

She said sleepily, 'What's the matter?' And then, 'Oh. Why, I wonder what they want.'

The ferry was coming in close, and on the hardstand several men were standing patiently, behind them a police popper, its blades still but its official-business light winking red. In the floodlights that revealed the landing X to the pilot, Cornut vaguely recognized one of the men, an administration staffer; the others all wore police uniforms.

'I wonder,' he said, glad that he didn't have to explain the shudder. 'Well, I'll sleep well tonight.' He took her hand and helped her, unnecessarily but pleasurably, down the steps.

A squat uniformed man stepped forward. 'Master Cornut? Sergeant Rhame. You won't remember me, but – '

Cornut said, 'But I do. Rhame. You were in one of my classes, six or seven years ago. Master Carl recommended you; in fact, he was your advocate at the orals for your thesis.'

There was a pause. 'Yes, that's right,' said Rhame. 'He wanted me to apply for the faculty, but I'd majored in Forensic Probabilistics and the Force had already accepted me, and – Well, that's a long time ago.'

Cornut nodded pleasantly. 'Good to see you again, Rhame. Good night.' But Rhame shook his head.

Cornut stopped, a quick, vague fear beginning to pulse in his mind. No one enjoys the sudden knowledge that the policeman in front of him wants to discuss official business; Rhame's expression told Cornut that that was so. He said sharply, 'What is it?'

Rhame was not enjoying himself. 'I've been waiting for you. It's about Master Carl; you're his closest friend, you know. There are some questions – '

Cornut hardly noticed Locille's sudden, frightened clutching at his arm. He stated, 'Something's happened to Carl.'

Rhame spread his hands. 'I'm sorry. I thought you knew. The lieutenant sent word to have you called from the texas; probably you'd left before the message got there.' He was trying to be kind, Cornut saw. He said, 'It happened about an hour ago – around twelve o'clock. The President had gone to bed – St Cyr, I mean. Master Carl came storming into his residence – very angry, the housekeeper said.'

'Angry about what?' shouted Cornut.

'I was hoping you could tell us that. It must have been something pretty serious. He tried to kill St Cyr with an axe. Fortunately – ' He hesitated, but could find no way to withdraw the word. 'As it happened, that is, the President's bodyguard was nearby. He couldn't stop Master Carl any other way; he shot him to death.'

Chapter Eleven

Cornut went through that night and the next day in a dream. It was all very simple, everything was made easy for him, but it was impossibly hard to take. Carl dead! The old man shot down – attempting to commit a murder! It was more than unbelievable, it was simply fantastic. He could not admit its possibility for a second.

But he could not deny.

Locille was with him almost every moment, closer than a wife need be, even closer than a watchdog. He didn't notice she was there. He would have noticed if she were missing. It was as though she had always been there, all his life, because his life was now something radically new, different, something that had begun at one o'clock in a morning, stepping out of a ferry popper to see Sergeant Rhame.

Rhame had asked him all the necessary questions in a quarter of an hour, but he had not left him then. It was charity, not duty, that kept him. A policeman, even a forensic probabilistician detailed to Homicide at his own personal request, is used to violence and unlikely murderers, and can sometimes help to explain difficult facts to the innocent bystanders. He tried. Cornut was not grateful. He was only dazed.

He cancelled his classes for the next day – tapes would do – and accompanied Rhame on a laborious retracing of Carl's last moves. First they visited St Cyr's residence and found the President awake and icy. He did not seem shaken by his experience; but then, he never did. He gave them only a moment of his time. 'Carl a kill-er. It is a great shock, Cor-nut. Ge-ni-us, we can not ex-pect it to be sta-ble, I sup-pose.' Cornut did not want to linger. St Cyr's presence was never attractive, but the thing that repelled him about the interview was the sight of the fifteenth-century halberd replaced on the floor where, they said, Master Carl had dropped it as the gunman shot him down. The pile of the carpet there was crisper, cleaner than the rest. Cornut was sickly aware that it had been cleaned, and aware what stain had been so quickly dissolved away.

He was glad to be out of the President's richly furnished residence, though the rest of the day was also no joy. Their first stop was the night proctor on Carl's floor, who confirmed that the house master had left at about ten o'clock, seeming disturbed about something but, in his natural custom, giving no clue as to its nature to an undergraduate. As it did not occur to them to question the aborigines, they did not learn of his brief and entirely one-sided conversation, but they picked up his trail at the next point.

Master Carl had turned up at the stacks at twenty-five minutes past ten, demanding instant service from the night librarian.

The librarian was a student, working off part of his tuition, as most students did. He was embarrassed, and Cornut quickly deduced why. 'You were asleep, weren't you?'

The student nodded, hanging his head. He was very nearly asleep talking to them; the news of Master Carl's death had reached every night clerk on the campus, and the boy had been unable to get to sleep. 'He gave me five demerits, and – ' He stopped, suddenly angry with himself.

Cornut deduced the reason. 'Consider them cancelled,' he said kindly. 'You're quite right in telling us about them. Sergeant Rhame needs all the information.'

'Thank you, Master Cornut. I – uh – I also didn't have a chance to get the ashtray off my desk, and he noticed it. But he just said he wanted to use the stacks.' The undergraduate waved towards the great air-conditioned hall where the taped and microfilmed University Library was kept. The library computer was served by some of the same circuits as the Student Test-Indices (College Examinations) Digital Computer on the level above it; all the larger computers on the campus were cross-hooked to some degree.

Rhame was staring at the layout. 'It's got more complicated since I was here,' he said. 'Did Master Carl know how to use it?'

The student grinned. 'He thought he did. Then he came storming back to me. He couldn't get the data he wanted. So I tried to help him – but it was classified data. Census figures.'

'Oh,' said Cornut.

Sergeant Rhame turned and looked at him. 'Well?'

Cornut said, 'I think I know what he was after, that's all. It was the Wolgren.'

Rhame understood what he was talking about – fortunately, as it had not occurred to Cornut that anyone would fail to be aware of Wolgren's Distributive Law. Rhame said, 'I only use some special Wolgren functions; I don't see exactly what it has to do with census figures.'

Cornut sat down, beginning to lecture. Without looking he put out his hand and Locille, still with him, took it. 'It's not important to what you're looking for. Anyway, I don't *think* it is. We had a question up for study – some anomalies in the Wolgren distribution of the census figures – and, naturally, there shouldn't be any anomalies. So I took it as a part-time project.' He frowned. 'I thought I had it beaten, but I ran into trouble. Some of the values derived from my equations turned out to be .. ridiculous. I tried to get the real values, but I got the same answer as Master Carl, they were classified. Silly, of course.'

The student librarian chimed in, '*He* said moronic. He said he was going to take it up with the Saint –' He stopped, blushing.

Rhame said, 'Well, I guess he did. What were the values that bothered you?'

Cornut shook his head. 'Not important; they're wrong. Only I couldn't find my mistake. So I kept going over the math. I suppose Carl went through the same thing, and then decided to take a look at the real values in the hope that they'd give some clue, just as I did.'

'Let's take a look,' said Rhame. The student librarian led them to the library computer, but Cornut nodded him away. He set up the integrals himself.

'Age values,' he explained. 'Nothing of any great importance, of course. No reason it should be a secret. But – '

He finished with the keyboard, and indicated the viewer of the screen. It flickered, and then bloomed with a scarlet legend:

Classified Information

Rhame stared at the words. He said, 'I don't know.'

Cornut understood. 'I can't believe it, either. True, Carl was a house-master. He felt he had certain rights. ...'

The policeman nodded. 'What about it, son? Did he act peculiar? Agitated?'

'He was mad as hell,' said the student librarian with satisfaction. 'He said he was going right over to the Sa – to the President's residence and get clearance to receive the data. Said it was moronic – let's see – "moronic, incompetent bureaucracy",' he finished with satisfaction.

Sergeant Rhame looked at Cornut. 'Well, the inquest will have to decide,' he said after a moment.

'Do you think he would try to *kill* a man?' Cornut demanded harshly.

'Master Cornut,' said the policeman slowly, 'I don't think anybody ever really wants to kill anybody. But he blew his top. If he was angry enough, who knows?' He didn't give Cornut a chance to debate the matter. 'I guess that's all,' he said, turning back to the night librarian. 'Unless he said anything else?'

The student hesitated, then grinned faintly. 'Just one other thing. As he was leaving, he gave me ten more demerits for smoking on duty.'

The following morning Cornut was summoned to the Chancellor's office to hear the reading of Carl's will.

Cornut was only mildly surprised to find that he was Master Carl's sole heir. He was touched, however. And he was saddened, for Master Carl's own voice told him about it.

That was the approved way of recording the most important documents, and it was like Master Carl to believe that the disposition of his tiny estate was of great importance. It was a tape of his image that recited the sonorous phrases: 'Being of sound and disposing mind, I devise and bequeath unto my dear friend, Master

Cornut – ' Cornut sat blinking at the image. It was entirely lifelike. That, of course, was the point; papers could be forged and sound tapes could be altered, but there was no artisan in the world who could quite succeed in making a change in a video tape without leaving a trace. The voice was the voice that had boomed out of a million student television sets for decades. Cornut, watching, hardly listened to the words but found himself trying to tell when it was that Carl had made the decision to leave him all his worldly goods. The cloak, he recalled vaguely, was an old one; but when was it Carl had stopped wearing it?

It didn't matter. Nothing mattered about Master Carl, not any more; the tape rattled and flapped off the reel, and the picture of Master Carl vanished from the screen.

Locille's hand touched his shoulder.

The chancellor said cheerfully, 'Well, that's it. All yours. Here's the inventory.'

Cornut glanced over it rapidly. Books, more than a thousand of them, value fixed by the appraisers (they must have been working day and night!) at five hundred dollars and a bit. Clothing and personal effects – Cornut involuntarily grinned – an arbitrary value of $1. Cash on hand, a shade over a thousand dollars, including the coins in his pocket when he died. Equity in the University pension plan, $8,460; monthly salary due, calculated to the hour of death, $271; residuals accruing from future use of taped lectures, estimated, $500. Cornut winced. Carl would have been hurt by that, but it was true; there was less and less need for his old tapes, with newer professors adopting newer techniques. And there was an estimate of future royalties to be earned by his mnemonic songs, and that was unkindest of all: $50.

Cornut did not bother to read the itemized liabilities – inheritance tax, income tax due, a few miscellaneous bills. He only noted the net balance was a shade over $8,000.

The funeral director walked silently from the back of the room and suggested, rather handsomely, 'Call it eight thousand even. Satisfactory? Then sign here, Master Cornut.'

'Here' was at the bottom of a standard mortuary agreement, with the usual fifty-fifty split between the heirs and the mortician. Cornut signed quickly, with a feeling of slight relief. He was getting off very lightly. The statutory minimum fee for a basic funeral was $2500; if the estate had been less than $5,000, he would have inherited only the balance above $2500; if it had been under $2500, he would have had to make up the difference. That was the law. More than one beneficiary, legally responsible for the funeral expenses, had regretted the generous remembering of the deceased. (In fact, there were paupers in the world who sold their wills as an instrument of revenge on occasion. For a hundred dollars' worth of liquor they would bequeath their paltry all to the drink-supplier's worst enemy, who would then, sooner or later, find himself unexpectedly saddled with an inescapable $2500 cost.)

Sergeant Rhame was waiting for them outside the Chancellor's office. 'Do you mind?' he asked politely, holding out his hand. Cornut handed over the mortuary agreement, containing the inventory of Carl's estate. The policeman studied it thoughtfully, then shook his head. 'Not much money, but he didn't need much, did he? It doesn't help explain anything.' He glanced at his watch. 'All right,' he said. 'I'll walk over with you. We're due at the inquest.'

As a tribute to the University, the state medical examiner had empanelled a dozen faculty members as his jury. Only one was from the Mathematics Department, a woman professor named Janet, but Cornut recognized several of the others, vaguely, from faculty teas and walks on the campus.

St Cyr testified, briefly and in his customary uninflected pendulum-tick, that Master Carl had shown no previous signs of insanity but had been wild and threatening indeed the night of his death.

St Cyr's housekeeper testified the same, adding that she had feared for her own life.

The bodyguard who killed Carl took the stand. Cornut felt Locille shrink in the seat beside him; he understood; he felt the same revulsion. The man did not seem much different from other men, though; he was middle-aged, husky, with a speech impediment that faintly echoed St Cyr's own. He explained that he had been on President St Cyr's payroll for nearly ten years; that he had once been a policeman and that it was not uncommon for very wealthy men to hire ex-policemen as bodyguards; and that he had never before had to kill anyone in defence of St Cyr's life. 'But this one. He was dangerous. He was ... going to kill ... somebody.' He got the words out slowly, but without appearing particularly agitated.

Then there were a few others – Cornut himself, the night proctor, the student librarian, even the sex-writer, Farley, who said that Master Carl had indeed seemed upset on his one personal contact with him, but of course, the occasion had been a disturbing one; he had told him of Master Cornut's most recent suicide attempt. Cornut attempted to ignore the faces that turned towards him.

The verdict took five minutes: 'Killed in self-defence, in the course of attempting to commit murder.'

For days after that Cornut kept away from St Cyr's residence, for the sake of avoiding Carl's executioner. He had never seen the man before Carl was killed, and never wanted to see him again.

But as time passed, Carl's death dwindled in his mind; his own troubles, more and more, filled it.

As day followed day, he began to approach, then reached, finally passed the all-time record for suiciders. And he was still alive.

He was still alive because of the endless patience and watchfulness of Locille. Every night she watched him asleep, every morning she was up before him. She began to look pale, and he found her taking catnaps in the dressing-room while he was lecturing to his classes; but she did not complain. She also did not tell him, until he found the marks and guessed, that twice in one week, even with her alert beside him, he had severed his wrists, first on a letter opener, second on a broken drinking tumbler. When he chided her for not telling him, she kissed him. That was all.

He was having dreams, too, queer ones; he remembered them sharply when he woke, and for a while told them to Locille, and then stopped. They were very peculiar. They had to do with being watched, being watched by some gruff, irritated warden, or by a hostile Roman crowd waiting for his blood in the arena. They were unpleasant; and he tried to explain them to himself. It was because he was subconsciously aware of Locille watching him, he told himself; and in the next breath said, *Paranoia*. He did not believe it. . . . But what then? He considered returning to his analyst, but when he broached it to Locille she only looked paler and more strained. Some of the sudden joy had gone out of their love; and that worried Cornut; and it did not occur to him that the growing trust and solidarity between them was perhaps worth more.

But not all the joy had gone. Apart from interludes of passion, somewhat constrained by Locille's ironclad determination to stay awake until he was quite asleep, apart from the trust and closeness, there were other things. There was the interest of work shared, for as Cornut's wife Locille became more his pupil than ever before in one of his classes; together they rechecked the Wolgren, found it free of gross error, reluctantly shelved it for lack of confirming data and began a new study of prime distribution in very large numbers. They were walking back to the Math Tower one warm day, planning a new approach through analytic use of the laws of congruence, when Locille stopped and caught his arm.

Egerd was coming towards them.

He was tanned, but he did not look well. Part of it was for reasons Cornut had only slowly come to know; he was uncomfortable in the presence of the girl he loved and the man she had married. But there was something else. He looked sick. Locille was direct: 'What in the world's the matter with you?'

Egerd grinned. 'Don't you know about Med School? It's traditional, hazing freshmen. The usual treatment is a skin fungus that turns sweat rancid, so you stink, or a few drops of something that makes you break out in orange blotches, or – well, never mind. Some of the jokes are kind of, uh, personal.'

Locille said angrily, 'That's terrible. You don't look very funny to me, Egerd.'

Cornut said to her, after Egerd had left, 'Boys will be boys.' She looked at him swiftly. He knew his tone had been callous. He didn't know that she understood why;

he thought his sudden sharp stab of jealousy had been perfectly concealed.

A little over two weeks after Master Carl's death, the proctor knocked on Cornut's door to say that he had a visitor. It was Sergeant Rhame, with a suitcase full of odds and ends. 'Master Carl's personal effects,' he explained. 'They belong to you now. Naturally, we had to borrow them for examination.'

Cornut shrugged. The stuff was of no great value. He poked through the suitcase; some shabby toilet articles, a book marked *Diary* – he flipped it open eagerly, but it recorded only demerits and class attendances – an envelope containing photographic film.

Sergeant Rhame said, 'That's what I wanted to ask you about. He had a lot of photographic equipment. We found several packs of film, unopened, which Master Carl had pressed against some kind of radiation-emitting paint on a paper base. The lab spent a long time trying to figure it out. They guessed he was trying to get the gamma radiation from the paint to register on the film, but we don't know why.'

Cornut said, 'Neither do I, but I can make a guess.' He explained about Carl's off-duty interests, and the endless laborious work that he had been willing to put into them. 'I'm not sure what his present line was, but I know it had something to do with trying to get prints of geometrical figures – stars, circles, that sort of thing. Why? Do you mean he finally succeeded in getting one?'

'Not exactly.' Sergeant Rhame opened the package and handed Cornut a glossy print. 'All the negatives were blank except one. This one. Make anything of it?'

Cornut studied it. It seemed to be a photograph of a

sign, or a printer's proof. It was not very well defined, but there was no doubt what it said. He puzzled over it for a while, then shook his head.

The lettering on the print said simply:

YOU DAMN OLD FOOL

Chapter Twelve

The wind was brisk, and the stretched cables under the texas made a bull-roarer sound as they vibrated. The pneumatic generators rattled, whined and crashed. Locille's brother was too used to them to notice.

He wasn't feeling very well, but it was his custom to do what his parents expected him to do, and they expected that he would watch the University broadcasts of his sister's classes. The present class was Cornut's, and Roger eyed with polite ignorance the professor's closely-reasoned exposition of Wilson's Theorem. He watched the dancing girls and the animated figures with more interest, but it was, on the whole, a disappointing show. The camera panned the studio audience only twice, and in neither case was he able to catch a glimpse of Locille.

He reported to his mother, took his last look at the flag Locille had brought him, and went to work.

As the day wore on, Roger felt worse. First it was his head pounding, then his bones aching, then an irresistible sudden nausea. Roger's job was conducive to that; he spent the whole day standing thigh deep in a smelly fluid composed of salt water, fish lymph and blood.

Ordinarily it didn't bother him (as nothing much bothered him, anyhow). Today was different. He steadied himself with one hand against a steel-topped table, shook his head violently to clear it. He had just come back from a hasty trip to the washroom, where he had vomited profusely. Now it seemed he was close to having to race out there again.

Down the table the sorter called, 'Roger! *Hey*! You're holding up the works.'

Roger rubbed the back of his neck and mumbled something that was not intelligible, even to himself. He got back to work because he had to; the fish were piling up.

It was the sorter's job to separate the females of the stocked Atlantic salmon run from the males. The male fish were thrust down a chute to a quick and undistinguished death. But the females, in breeding season, contained something too valuable to be wasted on the mash of entrails and bony parts that made dry fish meal. That was Roger's job – Roger's and a few dozen others who stood at tables just like his. The first step was to grasp the flopping female by the tail with one hand and club her brains out, or as nearly as possible out, with the other. The second was to hold her with both hands, exposing her belly to his partner across the table, whose long, fat knife ripped open the egg sac inside. (Quite often the knife missed. Roger's job was not sought after.) A quick wringing motion; the eggs poured one way, the gutted body slid another; and he was ready for the next fish. Sometimes the fish struggled terribly, which was unpleasant for a man with imagination; even the dullest grew to dislike the work. Roger had held the same job for four years.

'Come on, Roger!' The sorter was yelling at him again. Roger stared at him woozily. For the first time he became suddenly aware of the constant *slam*, bang, rattle, *roar* that permeated the low-level fishery plant. He opened his mouth to say something; and then he ran. He made it to the washroom, but with nothing at all to spare.

An hour later, his mother was astonished to see him home. 'What happened?'

He tried to explain everything that had happened, but it involved some complicated words. He settled for 'I didn't feel good.'

She was worried. Roger was always healthy. He didn't look good, ever, but that was because the part of his brain that was damaged had something to do with his muscle tone; in fact, he had been sick hardly a week's total in his life. She said doubtfully, 'Your father will be home in an hour or so, but maybe I ought to call him. I wonder. What do you think, Roger?'

That was rhetoric; she had long since reconciled herself to the fact that her son did not think. He stumbled and straightened up, scowling. The back of his neck was beginning to pain badly. He was in no mood to contemplate hard questions. What he wanted was to go to bed, with Locille's flag by his pillow, so that he could fondle it drowsily before he slept. That was what he liked. He told his mother as much.

She was seriously concerned now. 'You *are* sick. I'd better call the clinic. You lie down.'

'No. No, you don't have to. They called over at the place.' He swallowed with some pain; he was beginning to shiver. 'Mr Garney took me to the dia – the dia –'

'The diagnosticon at the clinic, Roger!'

'Yes, and I got some pills.' He reached in his pocket and held up a little box. 'I already took one and I have to take some more later.'

His mother was not satisfied, but she was no longer

very worried; the diagnostic equipment did not often fail. 'It's that cold water you stand in,' she mourned, helping him to his room. 'I've told you, Roger. You ought to have a better job. Slicer, maybe even sorter. Or maybe you can get out of that part of it altogether. You've worked there four years now. . . .'

'Good night,' Roger said inappropriately – it was early afternoon. He began to get ready for bed, feeling a little better, at least psychologically, in the familiar, comfortable room with his familiar, comfortable bed and the little old Japanese flag wadded up by the pillow. 'I'm going to sleep now,' he told her, and got rid of her at last.

He huddled under the warming covers – set as high as the rheostat would go, but still not high enough to warm his shaking body. The pain in his head was almost blinding now.

At the clinic, Mr Garney had been painfully careful to explain what the pills were for. They would take away the pain, stop the throbbing, make him comfortable, let him sleep. Feverishly Roger shook another one out of the box and swallowed it.

It worked, of course. The clinic's pills always performed as advertised. The pain dwindled to a bearable ache, then to a memory; the throbbing stopped; he began to fall asleep.

Roger felt drowsily peaceful. He could not see his face, and therefore did not know how flushed it was becoming; he had no idea that his temperature was climbing rapidly. He went quite happily to sleep . . . with the old, frayed flag against his cheek . . . just as he had done for nearly three weeks now, and as he would never in this life do again.

The reason Roger hadn't seen his sister in the audience was that she wasn't there; she was waiting in Cornut's little dressing-room. Cornut suggested it. 'You need the rest,' he said solicitously, and promised to review the lesson with her later.

Actually he had another motive entirely. As soon as he was off the air, he wrote a note for Locille and gave it to a student to deliver:

There's something I have to do. I'll be gone for a couple of hours. I promise I'll be all right. Don't worry.

Before the note reached her, Cornut was at the bridge, in the elevator, on his way to the city.

He did have something to do, and he did not want to talk to Locille about it. The odd dreams had been worsening, and there had been other things. He nearly always had a hangover now, for instance. He had found that a few drinks at night made him sleep better and he had come to rely on them.

And there was something else, about which he could not talk to Locille at all because she would not talk.

The monotrack let him out far downtown, in a bright, noisy, stuffy underground station. He paused at a phone booth to check the address of the sex-writer, Farley, and hurried up to street level, anxious to get away from the smell and noise. That was a mistake. In the open the noise pounded more furiously, the air was even more foul. Great cubical blocks of buildings rose over him; small three-wheeled cars and large commercial vehicles pounded on two levels around him. It was only a minute's walk to Farley's office, but the minute was an ordeal.

The sign on the door was the same as the lettering on his folder:

The sex-writer's secretary looked very doubtful, but
finally reported that Mr Farley would be able to see
Master Cornut, even without an appointment. Cornut
sat across the desk, refused a cigarette and said directly,
'I've studied the sample scripts you left for us, Farley.
They're interesting, though I don't believe I'll require
your services in future. I think I've grasped the notation,
and I note that there is one page of constants which
seems to describe the personality traits of my wife and
myself.'

'Oh, yes. Very important,' said Farley. 'Yours is
incomplete, of course, as I had no real opportunity to
interview you, but I secured your personnel-file data,
the profile from the Med Centre and so on.'

'Good. Now I have a question to ask you.'

Cornut hesitated. The proper way to ask the question
was to say: I suspect, from a hazy, sleepy recollection,
that the other morning I made a rather odd suggestion
to my wife. That was the proper way, but it was embarrassing; and it also involved a probability of having to
explain how many rather odd things he had done, some
of them nearly fatal, in those half-waking moments. . . .
'Let me borrow a piece of paper,' he said instead, and
rapidly sketched in a line of symbols. Stating the problem
in terms of ♂ and ♀ made it vastly less embarrassing;
he shoved it across the desk to the sex-writer. 'What
would you say to this? Does it fit in with your profile of
our personalities?'

Farley studied the line and raised his eyebrows.
'Absolutely not,' he said promptly. 'You wouldn't think
of it; she wouldn't accept it.'

'You could say it was an objectionable thing?'

'*Master Cor*nut! Don't use moralistic terms! A couple's sex life is entirely a private matter; what is customary and moral in one place is –'

'Please, Mr Farley. In terms of our own morals – you have them sketched out on the profile – this would be objectionable?'

The sex-writer laughed. 'More than that, Master Cornut. It would be absolutely impossible. I know my data weren't complete, but this sort of thing is out of the question.'

Cornut took a deep breath. 'But suppose,' he said after a moment, 'I told you that I had proposed this to my wife.'

Farley drummed his fingers on the desk. 'I can only say that other factors are involved,' he said.

'Like what?'

Farley said seriously, 'You must be trying to drive her away from you.'

In the two blocks between Farley's office and the monotrack station entrance, Cornut saw three men killed; a turbotruck on the upper traffic level seemed to stagger, grazed another vehicle and shot through the guard rail, killing its driver and two pedestrians.

It was a shocking interpolation of violence into Cornut's academic life, but it seemed quite in keeping with the rest of his day. His own life was rapidly going as badly out of control as the truck.

You must be trying to drive her away from you.

Cornut boarded his train, hardly noticing, thinking hard. He didn't *want* to drive Locille away!

But he also did not *want* to kill himself, and yet there was no doubt that he had kept trying. It was all part of a pattern, there could be no doubt of its sum: He was trying to destroy himself in every way. Failing to end his life, that destroyer inside himself was trying to end the part of his life that had suddenly grown to mean most to him, his love for Locille. And yet it was the same thing really, he thought, for with Locille gone, Carl dead, Egerd transferred, he would have no one close to him to help him through the dangerous half-awake moments that came at least twice in every twenty-four hours.

He would not last a day.

He slumped back into his seat, with the first sensation of despair he had ever felt. One part of his mind said judgementally: It's too bad.

Another part entirely was taking in his surroundings; even in his depression, the novelty of being among so many non-University men and women made an impression. They seemed so tired and angry, he thought abstractedly; one or two even looked sick. He wondered if any of them had ever known the helplessness of being under siege from the most insidious enemy of all, himself.

But suppose Master Carl was right after all, said Cornut to himself, quite unexpectedly.

The thought startled him. It came through without preamble, and if there had been a train of rumination that caused it, he had forgotten its existence. Right? Right about what?

The P.A. system murmured that the next stop was his. Cornut got up absently, thinking. Right?

He had doubted that Master Carl had really tried to kill St Cyr. But the evidence was against him; the police lab had verified his fingerprints on the axe, and they could not have been deceived.

So suppose Carl really had picked up the weapon to split the old man's skull. Incredible! But *if* he had . . .

And *if* Carl had not merely gone into an aberrated senile rage. ...

Why then, said Cornut to himself, emerging from the elevator at the base of the Bridge pier and blinking at the familiar campus, why then perhaps he had a reason. Perhaps St Cyr needed killing.

Chapter Thirteen

Entering the room was like being plunged under the surface of the sea. The lights were blue-green, concealed and reflecting from blue-green walls. A spidery mural of blue and green lines covered one wall like a wave pattern; from boxes along the floor grating rose curving branches of pale plants from the hybridization farms, resembling the kelp of the mermaid forests.

The pelagic motif was not a matter of design, it was only that these shapes and these colours were those that most pleased and comforted President St Cyr. This was his room. Not his study, with its oak panels and ancient armour; not even the 'private' drawing-room where he sometimes entertained members of the faculty. This was the room he reserved for a very, very few.

Four of these few were present now. A fat man, gross arms quivering, turned himself around and said, 'When?' He said, 'Do you want us all?' He said, 'That's Jillson's job.' St Cyr grinned and, after a moment, his bodyguard said, 'No, I don't. Really. You enjoy it more than I do.' A woman in a preposterously young frock opened her thin-lipped mouth and cackled hilariously, as there was a knock on the door.

Jillson, the bodyguard, opened it and revealed St Cyr's thin, silent housekeeper with Master Cornut.

St Cyr, on a turquoise wing chair, raised a hand. Jillson took Master Cornut by the arm and led him in, the door behind him closing on the housekeeper. Master Cor-nut,' said St Cyr in his odd, uninflected voice. 'I have been wait-ing for you.' The old woman in the young dress laughed shrilly for no visible reason; the bodyguard smiled; the fat man chuckled.

Cornut could not help, even then, looking around this room where he had never been. It was cool – the air was kept a full dozen degrees under the usual room temperature Cornut liked. There was a muted muttering of music in the background, too low to distinguish a tune. And these people – were odd.

He ignored Jillson, the assassin of Master Carl, whom he remembered from the inquest. The fat man blinked at him. 'Sen-a-tor Dane,' said St Cyr. 'And Miss May Kerbs.'

Miss May Kerbs was the one who had laughed. She swayed over to Cornut, looking like a teen-age girl in her first party formal. 'We were talking about you,' she said shrilly and Cornut with a physical shock, recognized that this was no teen-ager. She suddenly resembled the woman from South America whom he had met on the Field Expedition; the features were not much alike, but their state of repair was identical. The face was a skull's face under the make-up. She was fifty if she was a day – no, seventy-five – no; she was older than that; she was older than he liked to think, for a woman who dressed like a brash virgin.

Cornut found himself grotesquely acknowledging the introductions. He could not take his eyes off the woman. Talking about him? What had they been saying.

'We knew you'd be here, pal,' said the assassin, Jillson, kindly. 'You think we murdered the kid.'

'The kid?'

'Master Carl,' explained Jillson. *He had a reason*, said a thought in Cornut's mind. Queerly, it came in the half-stammering accent of Jillson.

'But sit down, Mas-ter Cor-nut,' St Cyr gestured. Politely the woman plumped cushions of aqua and turquoise on a divan.

'I don't want to sit down!'

'No. But please do.' St Cyr's blue-tinged face was only polite.

The fat man wheezed, 'Too bad, youngster. We didn't want to goose him along. I mean, why bother? But he was a nuisance. Every year,' he explained sunnily, 'we get maybe half a dozen who really make nuisances of themselves, mostly like you, some like him. His trouble was going after the classified material in the stacks. Well,' he said severely, waving a fat finger, 'that material is classified for a reason.'

Cornut sat down at last because he couldn't help himself. It was not going at all as he had expected; they were not denying a thing. But to admit that they killed Carl to protect some unimportant statistic in the census figures? It made no sense!

The blonde floozie laughed shrilly.

'Forgive Miss Kerbs,' said the fat man. 'She thinks you are funny for presuming to judge whether or not our actions are sensible. Believe me, young man, they are.'

Cornut found that he was grinding his teeth. These one-sided conversations, the answers coming before the questions were spoken, these queer half-understood remarks. . . .

It was as though they were reading his mind.

It was as though they knew every thought he had.

It was as though they were – but that's impossible! He thought, no, it can't be! Carl proved it!

The damn old fool.

Cornut jumped. The thought was in the tones of the

fat man's wheeze, and he remembered where he had seen words like that before.

The fat man nodded, his chins pulsing like a floating jellyfish. 'We exposed his plate for him,' he chuckled. 'Oh, yes. It was only a joke, but we knew he would not live to make trouble over it. Once he had the Wolgren analysis, he would have to be helped along.' He said politely, 'Too bad, because we wanted him to publish his proof that telepathy was impossible. It is; quite true. For him. But not for us. And unfortunately, my young friend, not for you.'

Locille woke shivering, reaching out at once to Cornut's side of the bed; but he was not in it.

She turned on the room lights and scanned the nearest of the battery of clocks; one o'clock in the morning.

She got up, looked out of the window, listened at the hall door, turned on the broadcast radio, shook the speaker-mike of the University annunciator to make sure it was working, checked the telephone to see that it was not unhooked, sat down on the side of the bed and, finally, began silently to weep. She was frightened.

Whatever compulsion drove Cornut to try suicide had never before stricken him when he was wide-awake and in possession of his thoughts. Was that no longer true? But if it was still true, *why* had he gone off like that?

The radio was whispering persuasively its stream of news-bulletins: Strikes in Gary, Indiana, a wreck of a cargo rocket, three hundred cases of Virus Gamma in one twelve-hour period, a catastrophic accident between a nuclear trawler and a texas (she listened briefly, then relaxed) off the coast of Haiti. As it did not mention Cornut's name, she heard very little. Where could he be?

When the telephone sounded she answered it at once.

It was not Cornut; it was the rough, quick voice of a busy man. '– asked me to call. She is with your brother. Can you come?'

'My mother asked you to call?'

Impatiently: 'That's what I said. Your brother is seriously ill.' The voice did not hesitate. 'It is likely that he will die within the next few hours. Goodbye.'

Love said, No, stay, wait for Cornut; but it was her mother who had sent for her. Locille dressed swiftly.

She left urgent instructions with the night proctor on what to do when – not if; *when* – Cornut returned. Watch him asleep; keep the door open; check him every half hour; be with him when he wakes. 'Yes, ma'am,' said the student, and then, with gentleness, 'He'll be all right.'

But would he? Locille hurried across the campus, closing her mind to that question. It was too late for a ferry from the island. She would have to go to the Bridge, ride to the city, hope for a helipopper ferry to the texas from there. The Med Centre was bright with lights from many rooms; curious, she thought, and hurried by. In their wired enclosure, the aborigines were murmuring, not asleep. Curious again.

But suppose the proctor forgot?

Locille reassured herself that he would not forget; he was one of Cornut's own students. In any case, she had to take the chance. She was almost grateful that something had happened to take her away, for the waiting had been unbearable.

She walked by the President's residence without a glance; it did not occur to her that the fact that it, too, was lighted, was of any relevance to her own problems. In this she was wrong.

It was not until she was actually boarding the slow-arriving monotrack that realization of where she was going and why finally struck her. Roger! He was *dying.*

She began to weep, for Roger, for the missing Cornut, for herself; but there was no one else on the car to see.

At that moment, Cornut, sore-eyed, was picking himself up from the floor.

Over him stood Jillson, patient and jolly, holding a club wrapped with a wet cloth. Cornut was aching as he had never imagined he could. He mumbled, 'You don't have to hit me any more.'

'Per-haps we do,' said St Cyr from his blue-green throne. 'We do not like this, you know. But we must.'

'Speak for yourself,' said Jillson cheerfully, and the ancient blonde screeched with laughter. They were talking among themselves, Cornut realized; he could hear only the audible part, but they were joking, commenting ... they were having a fine old time, while this methodical maniac bludgeoned him black and blue.

The fat senator wheezed, 'Understand our position, Cornut. We aren't cruel. We don't kill you shorties for nothing. But we aren't human, and we can't be judged by human laws. ... All right, Jillson.'

The bodyguard brought the club around, and Cornut sank against cushions the thoughtful old blonde kept re-piling for him. What made it particularly bad was that the senator held a gun. The first time he was beaten he had fought, but then the senator had held him at gunpoint while Jillson methodically battered him unconscious. And all the time they kept talking!

St Cyr said mildly, 'Stop.'

It was time for another break. That had been the fifth beating in six or seven hours, and in between they had interrogated him. 'Tell us what you un-der-stand, Cornut.'

The club had taught him obedience. 'You are a worldwide organization,' he said obediently, 'of the next species after humanity. I understand that. You need to survive, and it doesn't matter if the rest of us don't. Through your telepathic abilities you can suggest suicide to some persons who have the power in a latent form –' *Thus.*

'An a-bort-ed form,' corrected St Cyr as Cornut struggled erect again after the blow.

He coughed, and saw blood on the back of his hand. But he only said, 'An aborted form. Like myself.'

'Abortions of mutations,' chuckled the senator. 'Unsuccessful attempts on the part of nature to create ourselves.'

'Yes. Abortions of mutations, unsuccessful attempts. That is what I am,' Cornut parroted. 'And – and you are able to suggest many things, as long as the subject has the – the abortive talent, and as long as you are able to reach his mind when it is not fully awake.'

The blonde said, 'Very good! You're a good learner, Cornut. But telepathy is only a fringe benefit. Do you know what it is that makes us *really* different?'

He cringed away from Jillson as he shook his head.

The bodyguard glanced at the woman, shrugged and said, 'All right, I won't hit him. Go ahead.'

'What it is that makes us different is our age, my dear boy.' She giggled shrilly. 'For example, I am two hundred and eighty-three years old.'

They fed him after a while and let him rest.

Although he ached in every cell, there was hardly a mark on him; that was the reason for the padding on the club. And that had a meaning too, Cornut thought painfully. If they didn't intend to mark him, then they realized that he would be seen. Which meant that, at least, they weren't going to kill him out of hand and dump his body in the sea.

Two hundred and eighty-three years old.

And yet she was not the oldest of the four of them; only Jillson was younger, a child of a century or so. The senator had been born while America was still a British colony. St Cyr had been born in de Gaulle's France.

The whole key had been in the restricted areas of the stacks, if he had only seen it; for the anomaly in the Wolgren application was not Wolgren's fault at all. What the data would have shown was a failure of some people to die. Statistically insignificant for thousands of years, that fraction had grown and grown in the last two or three centuries – since Lister, since Pasteur, since Fleming. They were immortal – not because they could not become diseased or succumb to a wound, but because they would not otherwise die.

And with the growth of preventive medicine, they had begun to assert their power. They had really very little. They were not wiser than the rest of humanity or stronger. Even their telepathy was, it seemed, only unique because the short-lived humans had not the time to develop it; it depended on intricate and slow-forming neuronic hookups; it was a sign of maturity, like puberty or facial hair. Everything that made them powerful was only the gift of time. They had money. (But who, given a century or two of compound interest, could not be as rich as he chose?) They had a tight-held closed corporation devoted to their mutual interests – which was only sensible. They had furthered many a war, for what greater boon than war is there to medical science? They had endowed countless foundations, for the surgery of the short-lived could help preserve their own infinitely more valuable lives. And they had only contempt for the short-lived who fed them, served them and made their lives possible.

They *had* to be a closed corporation. Even an immortal needs friends, and the ordinary humans could for them be nothing more than weekend guests.

Contempt ... and fear. There were, they told him, the Cornuts, who had a rudimentary telepathic sense, who could not be allowed to live to develop it. Suggest killing, and the short-lived one died; it was that easy. The sleeping mind can build a dream out of a closing door, a distant truck's exhaust. The half-awake mind can convert that dream into action. ...

He heard a shrill laugh and the door opened. Jillson came in first, beaming. 'No!' cried Cornut instinctively, bracing himself against the club.

Chapter Fourteen

Locille sat next to her mother in the hospital's cafeteria, grateful that at last they had found a place to sit down. The hospital on the texas was unusually busy, worried visitors occupying every inch of space in the waiting-room, the halls outside the reception area, even the glassed-in sundeck that hung over the angry waves and was normally used for the comfort of the patients during the day. It was very late, and the cafeteria should have been closed; but the hospital had opened it for coffee and very little else. Her mother said something but Locille only nodded. She hadn't heard. It was not easy to hear, with the loud bull-roarer *twangg* of the suspended cables from the texas droning at them. And she had, besides, been thinking mostly of Cornut.

There had been no fresh news from the night proctor on the phone; Cornut had not returned.

'He ate so well,' her mother said suddenly. Locille patted her hand. The coffee was cold, but she drank it anyhow. The doctor knew where to find her, she thought, though of course he would be busy. . . .

'He was the best of my babies,' said her mother.

Locille knew that it was very close to ending for her brother. The rash that baffled the medics, the fever that glazed his eyes – they were only the outward indicators of a terrible battle inside his motionless body; they were headlines on a newspaper a thousand miles away, saying 800 *Marines Die Storming Iwo*; they represented the fact of blood and pain and death, but they were not the fact itself. Roger was dying. The outward indicators had been controlled, but salve could only dry up the pustulant sores, pills could only ease his breathing, shots could only soothe the pain in his head.

'He ate so well,' said her mother, dreaming aloud, 'and he talked at eighteen months. He had a little elephant with a music box and he could wind it up.'

'Don't worry,' whispered Locille falsely.

'But we let him go swimming,' sighed her mother, looking around the crowded room. It was she, not Locille, who first saw the nurse coming towards them through the crowd, and she must have known as soon as Locille, from the look on the nurse's face, what the message was that she had for them.

'He was the tenth in my ward today,' whispered the nurse, looking for a private place to tell them and not finding it. 'He never regained consciousness.'

Cornut walked out of the residence, blinking. It was morning. 'Nice day,' he said politely to Jillson, beside him. Jillson nodded. He was pleased with Cornut. The kid wasn't going to give them any trouble.

As they walked Jillson 'shouted' in Cornut's mind. It was hard with these half-baked telepaths, he sighed; but it was part of his job. He was the executioner. He took Cornut's elbow – bodily contact helped a little, not much – and reminded him what he was supposed to do. *You need to die. You'll kill yourself.*

'Oh, yes,' said Cornut aloud. He was surprised. He'd promised, hadn't he? He bore no resentment for the beating. He understood that it had a purpose; the more dazed, the more exhausted he was, the surer their control of him. He had no objection at all to being under the control of four ancient immortals, since – he was.

You die, Cornut, but what difference does it make? Today, tomorrow, fifty years from now. It's all the same.

'That's right,' Cornut agreed politely. He was not very interested, the subject had been thoroughly covered, all night long. He noticed absently that there was a considerable crowd around the Med Centre. The whole campus seemed somehow uneasy.

They crossed under the shadow of the Administration Building and circled around it, towards Math Tower.

You will die, you know, 'shouted' Jillson. *One day the world will wake up and no Cornut. Put a stethoscope to his poor chest, no heart beats. The sound of a beating heart that you have heard every day of your life will never be heard again.* Cornut was embarrassed. These things were true; he did not mind being told them; but it was certainly rather immature of Jillson to take such evident pleasure in them. His thoughts came with a sort of smirk, like an adolescent gloating over a dirty picture.

The brain turns into jelly, chanted Jillson gleefully. *The body turns into slime.* He licked his lips, hot-eyed.

Cornut looked about him, anxious to change the subject. 'Oh, look,' he said. 'Isn't that Sergeant Rhame?'

Jillson pounded on: *The hangnail on your thumb that hurts now will dissolve and rot and moulder. Not even the pain will ever be thought of by any living human again. Your bed-girl, is there anything you put off telling her? You put it off too long, Cornut.*

'It is Sergeant Rhame. Sergeant!'

Damn, crashed a thought in Cornut's mind; but Jillson was smiling, smiling. 'Hello, Sergeant,' he said with his voice, his mind raging.

Cornut would have helped Jillson along if he had known how, but his half-dazed condition robbed him of enterprise. Too bad, he thought consolingly, hoping that Jillson would pick up the thought. I know St Cyr ordered you to stay with me until I was dead, but don't worry. I'll kill myself. I promise.

Sergeant Rhame was talking gruffly to Jillson about the mob at Med Centre. Cornut wished Rhame would go away. He understood that Rhame was a danger to the immortals; they could not be involved, with the same people, in too many violent deaths. Rhame had investigated the death of Master Carl at Jillson's hands; he could not now be allowed to investigate even the suicide of Master Cornut, when he had seen Jillson with him going to his death. Jillson would have to leave him now. Too bad. It was so *right*, Cornut thought, that he should die for the sake of preserving the safety of the immortals, as they were the future of humanity. He knew this; they had told him so themselves.

A word caught his attention: '– since the sickness began they've been mobbing every hospital,' said Sergeant Rhame to Jillson, waving at the mob before Med Centre.

'Sickness?' asked Cornut, diverted. He stared at the policeman. It was as though he had said, I've got to get some garlic, there are vampires loose tonight. Sickness was a relic of the dark ages. You had a headache or a queasy stomach, yes, but you went to the clinic and the diagnosticon did the rest.

Rhame grumbled, 'Where've you been, Master Cornut? Nearly a thousand deaths in this area alone. Mobs seeking immunization. What they were calling Virus Gamma. It's really smallpox, they think.'

'Smallpox?' Even more fantastic! Cornut knew the word only as an archeological relic.

'Accidents all over the city,' said Rhame, and Cornut

thought suddenly of the crash he had seen. 'Fever and rash and – oh, I don't know the symptoms. But it's fatal. The medics don't seem to have a cure.'

'Me disfella smellim,' said a voice from behind Rhame. 'Him spoilim fes distime. Plantim manyfella pox.' It was one of the aboriginals, quietly observing while Rhame's police erected barricades in front of their enclosure. 'Plantin mefella Mary,' he added sadly.

Rhame said: 'Understand any of it? It's English, if you listen close. Pidgin. He says they know about small-pox. I think he said his wife died of it.'

'Plantim mefalla Mary,' agreed the aboriginal.

Rhame said, 'Unfortunately, I think he's right. Looks like your Field Expedition brought a lot of trouble back with it; the focus of infection seems to vector from these people. Look at their faces.' Cornut looked; the broad, dark cheeks were waffled with old pitted scars. 'So we're trying to keep the mob from making trouble here,' said Sergeant Rhame, 'by putting a fence around them.'

Cornut was even more incredulous than before. Mob violence?

It was not really his problem . . . since he would have no more problems in the world. He nodded politely to Rhame, conspiratorially to Jillson, and moved on towards Math Tower. The aborigine yelled something after him – 'Waitimup mefella Masatura-san, he speak you!' – it sounded like. Cornut paid no attention.

Jillson 'yelled' after him too. *Don't forget! You must die!* Cornut turned and nodded. Of course he had to die. It was only right. . . .

But it was difficult, all the same.

Fortunately Locille was not in the room. Cornut felt,

and quelled, a swift reeling sense of horror at the thought of losing her. It was only an emotion, and he was its master.

Probably the pithecanthropus had had similar emotions he thought, casting about for a convenient way to die. It was not as easy as it looked.

He made sure his door was locked, thought for a moment, and decided to treat himself to a farewell drink. He found a bottle, poured, toasted the air and said aloud, 'To the next species.' Then he buckled down to work.

The idea of dying is never far from the mind of any mortal, but Cornut had never viewed it as anything up close in the foreground of his future. It was curiously alarming. Everybody did it, he reassured himself. (Well, almost everybody.) Babies did it. Old men fouled themselves, sighed and did it. Neurotics did it because of an imagined insult, or because of fear. Brave men did it in war. Virgins did it as the less undesirable alternative to a sultan's seraglio, so said the old stories. Why did it seem so hard?

As Cornut was a methodical man, he sat down at his desk and began to make a list, headed:

MEANS OF DEATH
1. Poison.
2. Slashed wrists.
3. Jumping from window. (Or bridge.)
4. Electrocution. ...

He paused. Electrocution? It didn't sound so bad, especially considering that he had already tried most of the others, nearly. It would be nice to try something new. He poured himself another drink to think about it, and began to hum. He was feeling quite peaceful.

'It's only right that I should die,' he said comfortably.

'Naturally. Are you listening, Jillson?' He couldn't tell, of course. But probably they were.

And maybe they were worried. That was a saddening thought; he didn't want the immortals to worry about him. 'I understand perfectly,' he said aloud. 'I hope you hear me. I'm in your way.' He paused, not aware that he had raised a lectorial finger. 'It is,' he said, 'like this. Suppose I had terminal cancer. Suppose St Cyr and I were in a shipwreck, and there was only one lifebelt. He has a life ahead of him, I have at best a week of pain. Who gets the lifebelt?' He shook the finger. 'St Cyr does!' he thundered. 'And this is the same case. I have a mortal disease, humanity. And it's their lives or mine!'

He poured another drink and decided that the truths that had been whipped into him were too great to lose. The sheet of paper with suicide possibilities fell unheeded to the floor; humming, he wrote:

We are children and the immortals are fully grown. Like children, we need their knowledge. They lead us, they direct our universities and plan our affairs; they have the wisdom of centuries and without them we would be lost, random particles, statistical chaos. But we are dangerous children, so they must remain secret and those who guess must die. . . .

He crumpled the piece of paper angrily. He had nearly spoiled everything! His own vanity had almost revealed the secret he was about to die to protect. He scrambled on the floor for the list of possibilities, but stopped himself, bent over, staring at the floor.

The truth was that he didn't really like any of them.

He sat up and poured a drink sadly. He couldn't rely on himself to do a good job, he said to himself. Slashing his wrists, for example. Someone might come; and what could be more embarrassing than waking up on an operating table with sutures in his veins and the whole damned thing to do over again?

He noticed that his glass was again empty, but didn't bother to refill it. He was feeling quite sufficiently alcoholic already. If it weren't for his own confounded ineptitude he could be feeling pretty good, in fact, for it was nice to know that in a very short time he would be serving the best interests of the world by dying. Very nice. . . . He got up and wandered to the window, beaming. Outside the mobs were still swarming, trying to get immunization at the Med Centre; poor fools; he was *so* much better off than they! 'Strike the Twos and strike the Threes,' he sang. 'The Sieve of – Say!'

He had an idea. How fine it was, he thought gratefully, to have the wise helping hand of an elder friend in a time like this. He didn't have to worry about how to die, or whether he'd make a mess of it. He needed only to give St Cyr and the others a chance. Just relax . . . let himself get drowsy . . . even more drunk, perhaps. They would do the rest.

'The Sieve of Eratosthenes,' he sang cheerfully. 'When the multiples sublime, the numbers that are left, are prime!' He stumbled over to his bed and sprawled. . . .

After a moment he got up, angrily. He wasn't being a bit fair. If it was difficult for him to find a convenient way of dying in his room, why should he impose that difficulty on his good liege, St Cyr?

He was extremely irritated with himself over that; but, picking up the bottle, marching out into the hall, singing as he looked for a conveniently fatal spot, he gradually began to feel very good again.

Sergeant Rhame tested the barricades in front of the

aborigines' enclosure and let his men go back to trying to control the mobs at Med Centre. All the time his men were working, the aborigines had been trying to talk to them in their odd pidgin, but the police were too busy. The one who spoke English at all well, Masatura-san, was in his hut; the others were almost incomprehensible. Rhame glanced at his watch and decided that he had time for a quick cup of coffee before going over to help his men with the crowd. Although, he thought, it might be kinder to leave the crowd alone to crush half its members to death. At least it would be quick. And the private information of the police department surgeon was that the inoculations were not effective. .... He turned, startled, as a girl's voice called him.

It was Locille, weeping. 'Please, can you help me? Cornut's gone, and my brother's dead, and – I found this.' She held out the sheet with Cornut's carefully lettered list of suicide possibilities.

The fact that Rhame had been taken from his computer studies to help hold a mob down was evidence enough that he really belonged there; but he hesitated and was lost. Individual misery was that much more persuasive than mass panic. He began with the essentials: 'Where is he? No idea at all? No note? Any witnesses who might have seen him go? ... You didn't ask? *Why –*' But he had no time to ask why she had failed to question witnesses; he knew that every moment Cornut was off by himself was very possibly the moment in which he would die.

They found the student proctor, jumpy and distracted but still somewhere near his post. And he had seen Cornut!

'He was kind of crazy, I thought. I tried to tell him something – you know Egerd, used to be in his class?' (He knew perfectly just how well Locille had known

135

Egerd.) 'He died this morning. I thought Master Cornut would be interested, but he didn't even hear.'

Rhame observed the expression on Locille's face, but there was no time to worry about her feeling for a dead undergraduate. 'Which way? When?'

He had gone down the corridor more than half an hour before. They followed.

Locille said miserably, 'It's a miracle he's alive at all! But if he lasted this long ... and I was just a few minutes late ...'

'Shut up,' the policeman said harshly, and called out to another undergraduate.

Following him was easy; he had been conspicuous by his wild behaviour, even on that day. A few yards from the faculty refectory they heard raucous singing.

'It's Cornut!' cried Locille, and raced ahead. Rhame caught her at the door of the kitchens where she had worked so many months.

He was staggering about, singing in a sloppy howl one of Master Carl's favourite tunes:

> Add ray to modul, close th' set
> To adding, subtracting–

He stumbled against a cutting table and swore good-naturedly.

> Produce a new system, an' this goddam thing
> ... Is gen'rally termed a (*hic*) ring!

In one hand he had a sharp knife, filched from the meat-cutter's drawer; he waved it, marking time.

'Come on, damn it!' he cried, laughing. 'Goose me along!'

'Save him!' cried Locille, and started to run to him; but Rhame caught her arm. 'Let go of me! He might cut his throat!'

He held her, staring hard. Cornut didn't even hear them; he was singing again. Rhame said at last, 'But he isn't doing it, you see. And he's had plenty of time, by the look of the place. Suicidal? Maybe I'm wrong, Locille, but it looks to me as if he's just blind drunk.'

Chapter Fifteen

Throughout the city and the world there were scenes like the one in front of Med Centre, as a populace panicked by the apparition of pestilence – vanished these centuries! – scrambled for the amulet that would guard them against it. Hardly one man in a hundred was seriously ill, but that was enough. One per cent of twelve billion is a hundred and twenty million – a hundred and twenty million cases of the most deadly, most contagious ... and least excusable ... disease in medicine. For smallpox can infallibly be prevented, and only a world which had forgotten Jenner could have been taken by it unawares ... or a world in which the memory of Jenner's centuries-old prophylaxis had been systematically removed.

In the highest tower of Port Monmouth the eight major television networks shared joint transmitter-repeater facilities. Equatorially mounted wire saucers scanned the sky for the repeater satellites. As each satellite in its orbit broke free of the horizon, a saucer hunted and found it. That saucer clung to it as it traversed the sky, breaking free and commencing the search pattern for a new one as the old one dipped beneath the curve of the earth again. There were more than sixty satellites circling the earth which the repeaters could use, each one specially launched and instrumented to receive, clean, amplify and rebroadcast the networks' programmes.

Sam Gensel was senior shift engineer for the all-network technical crew at Port Monmouth.

It was not up to him to go out and get the pictures, to stage the shows or to decide what image went out on the air. Lecturing math professors, dimple-kneed dancers, sobbing soap-opera heroines – he saw all of them on the banked row of monitors in his booth. He saw all of them; be saw none of them. They were only pictures. What he really liked was test patterns, as they showed more of what he wanted to see. He watched for ripples of poor phasing, drifts off centre, the electronic snowstorm of line failure. If the picture was clear, he hardly noticed what it represented . . . except tonight.

Tonight he was white-faced.

'Chief,' moaned the rabbity junior engineer from Net Five, 'it's all over the country! Sacramento just came in. And the relay from Rio has a local collect that shows trouble all over South America.'

'Watch your monitor,' Gensel ordered, turning away. It was very important that he keep a clear head, he told himself. Unfortunately the head that he had to keep clear was aching fiercely.

'I'm going to get an aspirin,' he growled to his line man, a thirty-year veteran whose hands, tonight, were trembling. Gensel filled a paper cup of water and swallowed two aspirins, sighed and sat down at the coffee-ringed desk in the office he seldom had time to use.

One of the monitors showed an announcer whose smile was desperate as he read a newscast: '– disease fails to respond to any of the known antibiotics. All persons are cautioned to stay indoors as much as possible. Large gatherings are forbidden. All schools are closed until further notice. It is strongly urged that even within families personal contact be avoided as much as possible. And, above all, the Department of Public Health urges that everyone wait until an orderly programme of immunization can be completed. ....'

Gensel turned his back on the monitor and picked up the phone.

He dialled the front office. 'Mr Tremonte, please. Gensel here. Operational emergency priority.'

The girl was businesslike and efficient (but did her voice have a faint hysterical tremor?). 'Yes, sir. Mr Tremonte is at his home. I will relay.' Click, click. The picture whirred, blurred, went to black.

Then it came on again. Old man Tremonte was slouched at ease in a great leather chair, staring out at him irritably; the flickering light on his face showed that he was sitting by his fireplace. 'Well? What's up, Gensel?'

That queer, thin voice. Gensel had always, as a matter of employee discipline, stepped down hard on the little jokes about the Old Man – he had transistors instead of tonsils; his wife didn't put him to bed at night, she turned him off. But there was something definitely creepy about the slow, mechanical way he talked; and that old, lined face!

Gensel said rapidly, 'Sir, every net is carrying interrupt news bulletins. The situation is getting bad. Net Five cancelled the sports roundup, Seven ran an old tape of Bubbles Brinkhouse – the word is he's dying. I want to go over to emergency procedure. Cancel all shows, pool the nets for news and civil-defence instructions.'

Old man Tremonte rubbed his thin, long nose and abruptly laughed, like a store-window Santa. 'Gensel, boy,' he rasped. 'Don't get upset over a few sniffly noses. You're dealing with an essential public service.'

'Sir, there are *millions* sick, maybe dying!'

Tremonte said slowly, 'That leaves a lot who aren't. We'll continue with our regular programmes, and Gensel, I'm going away for a few days; I expect you to be in charge. I do not expect you to go over to emergency procedure.'

I never got a chance to tell him about the remote from Philadelphia, thought Gensel despairingly, thinking of the trampled hundreds at the Municipal Clinic.

He felt his warm forehead and decided cloudily that what he really needed was a couple more aspirin ... although the last two, for some reason, hadn't agreed with him. Not at all. In fact, he felt rather queasy.

Definitely queasy.

At the console the line man saw his chief gallop clumsily towards the men's washroom, one hand pressed to his mouth.

The line man grinned. Fifteen minutes later, though, he was not grinning at all. That was when the Net Three audio man came running in to report that the chief was passed out cold, breathing like a broken-down steam boiler, on the washroom floor.

Cornut, with black coffee in him, was beginning to come back to something resembling normal functioning. He wasn't sober; but he was able to grasp what was going on. He heard Rhame talking to Locille: 'What he really needs is massive vitamin injections. That would snap him right round – but you've seen what the Med Centre looks like. We'll have to wait until he sobers up.'

'I am sober,' said Cornut feebly, but he knew it was untrue. 'What happened?'

He listened while they told him what had been going on in the past twenty-four hours. Locille's brother dead,

Egerd dead, plague loose in the land . . . the world had become a different place. He heard and was affected, but there was enough liquor still in him and enough of the high-pressure compulsion exercised by the immortals so that he was able to view this new world objectively. Too bad. But – he felt shame – *why* had he failed to kill himself?

Locille's hand was in his, and Cornut, looking at her, knew that he never wanted to let it go again. He had not died when he should have. Now . . . now he wanted to live! It was shameful, but he could not deny it.

He still felt the liquor in him, and it gave the world a warm, fresh appearance. He was ashamed, but the feeling was remote; it was a failure of his childhood, bad, but so long ago. Meanwhile he was warm and comfortable. 'Please drink some more coffee,' said Locille, and he was happy to oblige her. All the stimuli of twenty-four full hours were working on him at once, the beating, the strain, the compulsion of the immortals. The liquor. He caught a glimpse of Locille's expression and realized he had been humming.

'Sorry,' he said, and held out his cup for more coffee.

Around the texas the waves were growing higher. The black barges tossed like chips.

Locille's parents braved the wind-blown rain topside to witness the solemn lowering of their son's casket into the black-decked funeral barge. They were not alone – there were dozens of mourners with them, strangers – and it was not quiet. *Dwang-g-g* went the bullroarer vibration of the steel cables. Hutch-*chumpf*, hutch-*chumpf* the pneumatic pens in the tower's legs caught trapped air from the waves and valved it into the pressure tanks for the generators. The noise nearly drowned out the music.

It was the custom to play solemn music at funerals, from tapes kept in the library for the purpose. The bereft were privileged to choose the programmes – hymns for the religious, Bach chorales for the classicists, largos for the merely mourning. Today there was no choice. The audio speakers played without end, a continuous random selection of dirges. There were too many mourners watching their children, parents or wives being awkwardly winched on to the tossing barges, on their way to the deep-sea funerary drop.

Six, seven . . . Locille's father carefully counted eight barges lying along the texas, waiting to be loaded. Each one held a dozen bodies. It was a bad sickness, he thought with detachment, realizing that the mourners were so few because, often enough, whole families were going to the barge together. He rubbed the back of his neck, which had begun to hurt. The mother standing beside him neither thought nor counted, only wept.

As Cornut sobered, he began to view his world and his past day in harsher, clearer perspective. Rhame helped. The policeman had the scraps of paper Cornut had left and he was remorseless in questioning. '*Why* must you die? *Who* are the immortals? *How* did they make you try to kill yourself – and why didn't you just now, with every chance in the world?'

Cornut tried to explain. To die, he said, remembering the lesson that had come with the beating, that is nothing; all of us do it. It is a victory in a way, because it makes death come to us on our terms. St Cyr and the others, however –

'St Cyr's gone,' rasped the policeman. 'Did you know

that? He's gone and so is his bodyguard. Master Finloe from Biochemistry is gone; and his secretary says he left with Jillson and that old blonde. Where?'

Cornut frowned. It was not in keeping with his concept of immortality that they should flee in the face of a plague. Supermen should be heroic, should they not? He tried to explain that, but Rhame pounced on him. 'Super-murderer, you mean! Where did they go?'

Cornut said apologetically, 'I don't know. But I assure you that they had reasons.'

Rhame nodded. His voice was suddenly softer. 'Yes, they did. Would you like to know what those reasons were? The aborigines brought that disease. They came off their island carrying active smallpox, nearly every one of them; did you know that? The worst active cases were brought, the well ones were left on the island. Did you know that? They were given injections – to cure them, they thought, but the surgeon says they were only cosmetic cures, the disease was still contagious. And they were flown to every major city in the world, meeting thousands of people, eating with them, in close contact. They were coached,' said Rhame, his face working, 'in the proper behaviour in civilized society. For example, the pipe of peace isn't their custom; they were told it would please us. Does that add up to anything for you?'

· Cornut leaned forward, his head buzzing, his eyes on Rhame. Add up? It added up; the sum was inescapable. The disease was deliberately spread. The immortals had, in their self-oriented wisdom, determined to move against the short-lived human race, in a way that had nearly destroyed it more than once in ancient days: they had spread a fearsome plague.

Locille screamed.

Cornut realized tardily that she had been drowsing

against his shoulder, unable to sleep, unable, after the sleepless night, to stay fully awake. Now she was sitting bolt upright, staring at the tiny glittering manicure scissors in her hand. 'Cornut!' she cried, 'I was going to stab you in the throat!'

It was night, and outside the high arch of the Bridge was a line of colour, the lights of the speedy monotracks and private vehicles making a moving row of dots.

On one of the monotracks the motorman was half listening to a news broadcast: 'The situation in the midwest is not as yet critical, but a wave of fear has spread through all the major cities of Iowa, Kansas and Nebraska. In Omaha more than sixty persons were killed when three heli-buses bearing emigrants collided in a bizarre mid-air accident, apparently caused by pilot error in one of the chartered planes. Here in Des Moines all transportation came to a halt for nearly ninety minutes this morning as air-control personnel joined the fleeing throngs, leaving their posts unattended. In a statement released –'

The motorman blinked and concentrated on his controls. He was fifty years old, had held this job and almost this run for more than half his life. He rubbed the sensor collar irritably; he had worn it nearly thirty years, but tonight it bothered him.

The collar was like a dead-man's switch, designed to monitor temperature and pulse, electronically linked to cut the monotrack's power and apply the brakes in the event of death or serious illness to the motorman. He was quite used to wearing these collars and appreciated the need for them; but tonight, climbing the approach ramp to the Bridge in third speed, his throat began to feel constricted.

Also his head ached. Also his eyes itched and burned. He reached for the radiomike that connected him to the dispatcher's office, and croaked, 'Charley, I think I'm going to black out. I –' That was all. No more. He fell forward. The sensors around his neck had marked his abnormal pulse and respiration for minutes, and reacted as he collapsed. The monotrack stopped dead.

Behind it another one drove catastrophically into its tail.

The motorman of the second unit had been feeling queasy for more than an hour and was anxious to get to the end of his run; he had been overriding the automatic slow-down controls all the way across the Bridge. As he passed the critical parameters of sensor monitoring, his own collar switched off the power in his drive wheels; but by then it was too late; the wheels raced crazily against air. Even the sensor collars had not been designed to cope with two motorman-failures in the same second. White sparks flew from Bridge to water and died – great white sparks that were destroyed metal. The pile-up began. The sound of crashing battered at the campus of the University below. The Bridge stopped, its moving lights becoming a row of coloured dots with one great hideous flare of colour in the middle.

After a few moments distant ambulance sirens began to wail.

Cornut held the weeping woman, his face incredulous, his mind working. Locille trying to kill him? Quite insane!

But like the other insane factors in his own life, it was not inexplicable. He became conscious, rather late, of faint whispering thoughts in his own mind. He said to

Rhame, 'They couldn't reach me! They tried to work with her.'

'Why couldn't they reach you?'

Cornut shrugged and patted her shoulder. Locille sat up, saw the scissors and hurled them away. 'Don't worry, I understand,' he said to her, and to the policeman, 'I don't know why. Sometimes they can't. Like in the refectory kitchen, just now; they could have killed me. I even wanted them to; but they didn't. And once on the island, when I was blind drunk. And once – remember, Locille? – on the Bridge. Each time I was wide open to them, and on the Bridge they almost made it. But I stopped in time. Each time I was fuddled. I'd been drinking,' he said, 'and they should have been able to walk right in and take possession . . .' His voice trailed thoughtfully off.

Rhame said sharply, 'What's the matter with Locille?'

The girl blinked and sat up again. 'I guess I'm sleepy,' she said apologetically. 'Funny . . .'

Cornut was looking at her with great interest, not as a wife but as a specimen. 'What's funny?'

'I keep hearing someone talking to me,' she said, rubbing her face fretfully. She was exhausted, Cornut saw; she could not stay awake much longer, not even if she thought herself a murderer, not even if he died before her eyes. Not even if the world came to an end.

He said sharply, 'Talking to you? Saying what?'

'I don't know. Funny. "Me softspeak you-fella." Like that.'

Rhame said immediately, 'Pidgin. You've been with the aborigines.' He dismissed the matter and returned to Cornut, 'You were on the point of something, remember? You said sometimes they could get at you, sometimes not. Why? What was the reason?'

Cornut said flatly: 'Drinking. Each of those times I had been drinking!'

It was true! Three times he had been where death should have found him, and each time it had missed.

And each time he had been drinking! The alcohol in his brain, the selective poison that struck first at the uppermost level of the brain, reducing visual discrimination, slowing responses . . . it had deafened him to the mind voices that willed him to death!

'Smellim olefella bagarimop allfella,' Locille said clearly, and smiled. 'Sorry. That's what I wanted to say.'

Cornut sat frozen for a second.

Then he moved. The bottle he had carried with him, Rhame had thriftily brought back to the room. Cornut grabbed it, opened it, took a deep swallow and passed it to Locille. 'Drink! Don't argue, take a good stiff drink!' He coughed and wiped tears from his eyes. The liquor tasted foul; it would take little to make him drunk again.

But that little might save his life . . . Locille's life . . . it might save the world's!

Chapter Sixteen

Tai-i Masatura-san got up from his bed and walked to the strong new fence.

The crazy white people had not come up with dinner for them. It was getting very late, he judged, though the position of the stars was confusing. A few weeks ago, on his island, the Southern Cross, wheeling about the sky, was all the clock a man needed. These strange northern constellations were cold and unpleasant. They told him nothing he wanted to know, neither time nor direction.

His broad nostrils wrinkled angrily.

In order to become a tai-i he had had to become skilled in the art of reading the stars, among many other arts. Now that art was of no value, rendered useless by the stronger art of the white man. His gift of deepsmell, the reaching out with a part of his mind to detect truth or falsehood that made him a tribal magistrate, it had been voided by the old ones, who smelled so strongly and yet could baffle his inner nose.

He should never have trusted the softspeaking white man of great age, he thought, and spat on the ground.

His second in command moaned at the door of the hut.

In the creolized speech which served them better than the tribe's pidgin or Masatura-san's painful English, the man whimpered: 'I have asked them to come, but they do not hear.'

'One hears,' said Masatura-san.

'The old ones are softspeaking endlessly,' whined the sick man.

'I hear,' said Masatura-san, closing his mind. He squatted, looking at the stars and the fence. Outside the campus was still noisy, voices, vehicles, even so late at night.

He thought very carefully what he wanted to do.

Masatura-san was a tai-i because of strength and learning, but also because of heredity. When the Japanese off the torpedoed destroyer had managed to reach his island in 1944 they had found a flourishing community. The Japanese strain in Masatura-san's ancestry came only from that generation. Before that his forebears were already partly exotic. The twelve Japanese were not the first sailors to wash ashore. Once 'Masatura-san' had been 'Masterson.' English fathers and Melanesian mothers had produced a sturdy race – once the objecting male Melanesians had been killed off. The Japanese repeated the process with the hybrids they found, as the English had done before them, except for a few.

One of those few was the great-grandfather of Tai-i Masatura-san. He had been spared for exactly one reason: he was the chief priest of the community, and had been for nearly a century; the islanders would have died for him. Many of them did.

Three hundred years later, his third-generation off-spring had inherited some of his talents. One was 'deep smelling' – no sniff of the nostrils, but a different sense entirely. Another was age. Masatura-san himself was nearly a century old. It was the only thing he had managed to conceal from the owners of the strange soft-speak voices who had found him on his island, and promised him much if he would help them.

The 'deep smell' of the world beyond the barricade was very bad.

Tai-i Masatura-san thought carefully and made a decision. He moved over to the hut and poked his second in command with his foot. 'Speak along him-fella two-time again,' he ordered in pidgin. 'Me help.'

Cornut left his wife smiling laxly and sound asleep. 'I'll be back,' he whispered, and with Sergeant Rhame hurried out on to the campus. The wind was rising, and stars broke through scudding clouds. The campus was busy. Around the Med Centre hundreds of people still waited, not because they had hope of immunization – the fact that the vaccine was ineffective had been announced – but because they had nowhere else to go. Inside the Clinic, medics with white faces and red eyes laboured endlessly, repeating the same tasks because they knew no others. In the first hour they had discovered that the reference stacks had been looted of three centuries of epidemiology; they could not hope to replace them in finite time, but they could not help but try. Half the medics were themselves sick, ambulatory but doomed.

Cornut was worried, not for himself but for Locille. Thinking back to the Field Expedition, he remembered the shots that St Cyr himself had taken and felt it more than likely that everyone receiving them had been rendered immune to the smallpox. But what of Locille? She had had nothing.

He had already told Rhame about the shots, and Rhame had instantly reported to the police head-quarters; they would radio the island, try to locate the medics who had administered the vaccine. Neither of them was hopeful. The immortals would surely have removed all traces of what might halt their attack against the short-lived bulk of humanity.

But that thought had a corollary too: If the immortals had removed it, the immortals had it now.

They found the aborigines waiting for them. 'You called us,' said Cornut – it was a question; he still could not really believe in it – and Masatura-san nodded and reached for his hand.

Rhame blinked at them dizzily. Cornut had made him take three large drinks too – not because Rhame had shown any signs of being telepathic, only because Cornut was not sure. It seemed like a drunken vision, the math teacher linking hands with the squat brown man, wordless. But it was no vision.

After a moment Cornut released the islander's hand. Masatura-san nodded and, without a word, took the bottle from Cornut, drank deep, and passed it to his second in command, barely conscious on the ground behind him. 'Let's go,' said Cornut thickly, his eyes glazed. (It was hard to be just drunk enough!) 'We need a popper. Can you get one?'

Rhame reached into his pocket automatically and spoke briefly into his police radio before he asked questions. 'What's happened?'

Cornut wavered and caught his arm. 'Sorry. It's all the immortals. You were right; they imported the smallpox carriers – went to a lot of trouble. But this fellow here, he's a lot older than he looks. He can read minds too.'

The police radio squawked faintly. 'They'll meet us over near Med Centre,' Rhame said, putting it back in his pocket. 'Let's go.' He was already moving before he asked, 'But where are we going?'

Cornut was having difficulty walking. Everything was

moving so slowly, so slowly; his feet were like sausage-shaped balloons, he was wading through gelatine. He measured his movements carefully, in a drunken, painstaking effort at clarity; he did not dare get too drunk, he did not dare become sober. He said: 'I know where the immortals are. He told me. Not words – holding my hand, mind to mind; bodily contact helps. He didn't know the name of the place, but I can find it in the popper.' He stopped and looked astonished. He said, 'God, I *am* drunk. We'll need some help.'

Rhame said, stumbling over the words, 'I'm drunk too, but I figured that out for myself. The whole Emergency Squad is meeting us.'

The cleared space near the Med Centre was ideal for landing helipoppers, even though it was dotted now with prostrate figures, sick or merely exhausted. Rhame and Cornut heard the staccato bark and flutter of the helipoppers and stood at the edge of the clear space, waiting. There were twelve police poppers settling towards them; eleven poised themselves in air, waiting; the twelfth blossomed with searchlights and came on down.

In the harsh landing light, one of the recumbent figures near them pushed himself up on an elbow, mumbling. His eyes were wide, even in the blinding light. He stared at Cornut, his lips moving, and he cried faintly: 'Carriers!'

Rhame first realized the danger. 'Come on!' he cried, beginning to trot, lurching, towards the landing popper. Cornut followed, but others were walking feverishly. 'Carriers!' they cried, ten of them and then a dozen. It was like the birth of a lynch mob. 'Carriers! They did it to us! Get them!' Sick figures pushed themselves to their knees, hands clutched at them. Half a dozen men, standing in a knot, whirled and ran towards them. 'Carriers!'

Cornut began to run. Carriers? Of course they were not carriers; he knew what it was. It was St Cyr perhaps, or one of the others, unable to break through the barrier of alcohol to reach his own mind, working with the half-waking minds of the hopeless hundreds on the grass to attack and destroy them. It was quite astonishing, meditated one part of his mind with drunken gravity, that there were so many partial telepaths in this random crowd; but the other part of his mind cried Run, run!

Stones began to fly, and from fifty yards away, across the green, Cornut heard a sound that might have been a shot. But the popper was whirling its blades above them now; they boarded it and it lifted, leaving the sudden mob, wakened to fury, milling about below.

The popper rose to join the rest of the squad. 'That was just in time,' breathed Cornut to the pilot. 'Thanks. Now head east until –'

The co-pilot was turning towards him, and something in his eyes stopped Cornut. Rhame saw it as fast as he. As the co-pilot was reaching for his gun the police sergeant brought up his fist. Co-pilot went one way, the gun another. Sitting on the co-pilot, Cornut and Rhame stared at each other. They didn't have to speak; the communication that passed between them was not telepathic; they both came to the same conclusion at once. Cornut jumped for the gun, pointed it at the only other man in the popper, the pilot. 'This is an emergency popper, right? With medical supplies.'

Rhame understood at once. He leaped for the locker and broke out a half-litre of brandy in a sealed flask. He handed it to the pilot. 'Drink!' he ordered. Then: 'Get on the radio! Tell every man in the squad to take at least two ounces of brandy!'

It was, thought Cornut dizzily, a hell of a way to fight a war.

Chapter Seventeen

Rhame was only a sergeant, but the pilot of the lead popper was a deputy inspector. Once he had enough alcohol in his bloodstream to blot out the nagging drive of the immortals he took command. The other helipoppers questioned his orders, all right. But they obeyed.

The fleet sailed out over the bay, over the city, up towards the mountains.

Underneath them the city lay helpless. It was flat and quiet from above, but at ground level it was a giant killing-pen where blind mobs roamed in terror. A thousand feet over the terrified streets, Cornut could see the fires of wrecked vehicles, the little heaps of motionless bodies, the utter confusion that the plague had wrought. Worse than plague was the panic. The deputy inspector had told him that there were by now more than ten thousand reported deaths in the city, but only a fraction of them were from smallpox. Terror had slain the rest.

Cornut knew that that was what the immortals wanted.

They had kept their herd of contented, helpless, short-lived cattle long enough. The herd had prospered until it competed with its unseen owners for food and space. Like any good husbandmen, the immortals had decided to thin the herd out.

What could be more painless, for them, than a biological thinner? As myxomatosis had rid Australia of the rabbit pest, so smallpox could control the swarming human vermin that was dangerous to the immortals.

Sergeant Rhame said thickly, 'Bad weather up there. I don't suppose we can go around.' Behind them the poppers trailed in clear air, but ahead, over the mountains, were towering clouds.

Cornut shook his head. He only knew the way St Cyr had gone, as St Cyr had seen it with his own eyes and the old islander had relayed it to him. They would have to fight through the storm.

Cornut closed his eyes briefly. It was war to the death now, and he wondered what it would be like to kill a man. He could understand well enough the motives of St Cyr and the others, waging a jealous battle against every threat, striking down those who like himself might learn of their existence, defeating research that might give them away by concealing it. It was a constant defensive action, and he could understand, he could even in a way forgive, their need to remove the threat. He could forgive their attempts on his own life, he could forgive their try at destroying most of a world.

He could not forgive the threat to Locille. For she was exposed. A few would survive the plague in any event – a few always did – but Cornut was a mathematician, and he did not accept one chance in a million as a sporting gamble against odds.

All these years, he dreamed, and all the while immortals were directing humanity in directions they chose. No wonder the great strides in medicine, no wonder the constant grinding competition between manufacturers for luxuries and comforts. How would it be if the immortals were destroyed?

And yet, he thought, beginning to sober up, and yet wasn't there something in Wolgren about that? No, not

Wolgren. But somewhere in statistical theory. Something about random movements. The Brownian Movement of molecules? That had been on Master Carl's mind, he remembered. The drunkard's walk – the undirected progress that moved from a dead centre ever more slowly, asymptotically, yet never stopped. Straight-line progress was always to an end; if the immortals directed it, it could go only so far as they could conceive.

They were not the future, he realized with sharp clarity. No super-potent force was the future; a kennel-man could breed dogs only to his own specifications, he could not give the species the chance at free growth that could go on and on and endlessly on; and – *Cornut*, said a shrill, angry whine in his brain.

Panicky, he grabbed for the flask of medicinal brandy and blotted out the voice with a choking swallow.

The flask was getting low. They would have to hurry. They dared not get more sober.

Senator Dane stirred angrily and crackled an oath with his mind that sent ripples of laughter through the party. *Don't laugh, you damned fools!* he thought. *I've lost them again.*

'Sweety-heart,' caroled the ancient bobbysoxer from South America, Madam Sant'Anna, 'san fairy-ann. Don't cry.' A mental image of a fat weeping baby with Dane's face.

Pistols firing, Madam Sant'Anna skewered with a thousand swords, thought the senator.

Not me. 'What, me worry?' A giggle.

You'll laugh out of the other side of your face. An image of an unmarked grave. An obscene gesture from the senator; but, in truth, he wasn't really worried either. He cast out for Cornut's mind again, but not more than half-heartedly, and when he could not find it he projected a mental picture of a staggering, vomiting drunk that made them smile. The senator hurled a painful thought at one of the dark servants and cheerfully awaited the bringing of his candies.

Senator Dane never drank, but he had observed the shorties drinking, he knew what drinking could do. Sometimes the immortals got the same sort of selective release from alkaloids. Enough alcohol to blot out control, he was confident, would blot out the motor reflexes. They would pile up against a hill, they would crash into each other. Certainly they would never find this place – although Masatura-san's mind had been powerfully clear, and possibly there had been a leak, and – no. St Cyr himself had selected Masatura-san's tribe for the job of extermination. No one could conceal anything from St Cyr. And the place was quite unfindable.

It very nearly was. It had been a resort hotel at one time, used for conventions of the sort that are not meant to be public, pre-empted from a gangster who had in turn pre-empted it from its (more or less) legitimate builders. The gangster had been a nuisance, and the immortal who killed him had felt rather virtuous as he murdered a murderer.

The hotel no longer had roads leading to it, and there was no other habitation within twenty miles. *That* had been expensive; but the immortals had known this storm was brewing half a century before and expense was the least important factor in any of their plans. There was room for all of them, seventy-five immortals from all over the world, 'children' of sixty or sixty-five, the oldest of all a man who had been born in the reign of Caligula. (There were very few born before the twentieth century, because of the public-health contribution to their long-

evity; but those few seemed unwilling ever to die at all.)
There were women who, with repeated plastic surgery,
had managed to keep themselves in the general appearance, from a distance, of youth. There were visible
ancients, like St Cyr with his cyanosis and his scars, the
squat old Roman with his great recurring keloids, the
hairless, fat black man who had been born in slavery on
the estate of the king's governor of Virginia. Colour
made no difference to them, nor race nor age; the factor
that counted was power. They were the strongest in the
world, as they insured by killing off the weak.

They were, however, cowards. They flocked like wild
geese to favourable climates, away from Europe in the
early twentieth century, away from the Pacific during
the bomb tests of the 1950s. They left North Africa well
before the Israeli-Arab clashes, and none of them had
visited China since the days of the Dowager Empress.
Not one had seen an earthquake or a volcano at close
range – or at any rate, not after realizing what they
were; and every one had, for all his prolonged life,
surrounded himself with walls and with guards. They
were cowards. They had the avarice of the very rich.
There were drawbacks to their lives, but not such a
drawback as dying.

In the great hotel, staffed by Sudanese flown in a
decade earlier, completely out of touch with the world
around them and guarded from even chance contact
with a wanderer by a totally unfamiliar tongue, they
prepared to sit out the plague. Senator Dane wandered
among them, jovial but faintly worried. He annoyed
them. The undertone of worry was like a constant
mumble to them, irritating. They chaffed him about it,
in words of fifty languages (they knew them all) or in
thoughts, with gesture and tone. But he infected them all.

Fear is a relative thing. The man who is starving does not fear the sudden early frost that may destroy the crops. It is too late for that; he can only worry about what is close at hand. The well-fed man can worry years ahead.

The immortals could worry a full century ahead. They were Rockefellers of life, dispensing hours and days to the short-lived like dimes; they looked far into the future, and every distant pebble in their path was a mountain. Dane's worry was small and remote, but it was a worry. Suppose, mumbled the fear behind the jolly mask, that they do find our place here. True, they can't do much to us – we can destroy them with their minds, as we always have – but that is a nuisance. We would want to flee. This is our best place, but we have others.

Shut up, thought (or said, or gestured) the others.

He was interfering with their fun. The Roman was demonstrating a delicate balance of a feather on a soap-bubble (he was the strongest of them; it was hard to move physical objects with the mind, but with age it became possible).

But the fear said: We have lost them. They might be anywhere. (The bubble collapsed.) The fear said: Even if we flee, they are not stupid; they might search the house and find our own medics. And then – look then! Then they can end the plague and, with only a few of them dead, some five billion people will be looking for us seventy-five! (The feather floated to the ground. The immortals shouted at him peevishly.)

I'm sorry.

'Don't be sorry, you damn old fool,' cried Madam Sant'Anna, petulantly picturing him in an embarrassingly private blunder. The Roman picked up the image and added a third-century refinement.

But suppose they do get through, sobbed Dane.

'Go,' said St Cyr in his clock-tick voice, angry enough to speak aloud, 'de-stroy the ser-um. Do not spoil our day!'

Unwillingly Dane went, his mumbling worry diminishing in their minds with distance. It stopped abruptly, and cheerfully the immortals returned to their pleasures. ... It stopped abruptly for Dane too.

He was in the downstairs hall, searching for one of the Sudanese servants, when he heard a sound behind him. He started to turn. But he was fat and he was, in spite of everything, very old.

The blow caught him and he fell heavily, like a bladder filled with lard. He was only vaguely conscious of the hands that rolled him over, the acrid taste of the something – was it liquor? But he *never* drank liquor! – they were forcing down his throat.

'Got one,' said one of the helicops thickly, staggering slightly.

Senator Dane did not know, but there were a dozen reeling figures around him, and more coming in. As he began to recover consciousness he knew, but then it was too late. It was so *still*. The voices in his mind were silent!

The alcohol was a barrier. It deafened him, blinded him, marooned him. He had only eyes and mouth and ears, and for one whose life had been illuminated by the rapid flash of the mind itself, that is blindness. He began to sob.

Cornut passed the kitchen where the servants huddled under guard and Senator Dane lay on the floor, and hurried after the helicops. He heard gunfire and felt a queasy panic. This was the moment of truth; in a few seconds now the world would change its complexion for ever, a pastured herd with immortals fattening on its bounty or a brawl of leaderless billions – *No*. He had not thought that! And in a flash he was in another mind; it was a seepage from the cranky petulance of St Cyr that had touched him then, so close and so strong that even battle and alcohol could not quite subdue it; what he had felt was what St Cyr felt.

Cornut began to run. It was like being in two places at once; he saw the police coming in, shooting; he ran behind them.

The immortals resisted as best they could, but their weapons were no longer appropriate. They were like billionaires trying to buy off a charging rhino or a Hitler attempting to sway an earthquake to his will. They could not prevail against this naked force, they could only die or be taken; and the blurred fury of their minds was like a shout or a stench.

He caught one last clear thought from St Cyr: *We lose*. There was no other. St Cyr was dead; and all about him police were overpowering the survivors.

Chapter Eighteen

Cornut passed out completely on the way back, and slept soddenly for hours. Rhame let him sleep. There was time enough for everything now, even for sleep. The medics, with the restored tapes for the stacks, had already begun the task of preparing vaccine; the hundred litres of serum was already being rationed among the already ill. The mobs were quieted – it took only hope to end their rage – and the danger, for most, was past. Not for all. The serum would never reach South Africa in time for some, for instance; and there were many already dead. But the dead were only in the millions. . . .

Cornut woke up like an explosion.

His head was pounding; he staggered to his feet, ready to fight. Rhame, full of wake-up pills but obviously fading, reassured him quickly. 'It's all right. Look!' They were back in the city, in a hastily cleared penal wing of one of the hospitals. Along a corridor, in room after room, there were couples of old, old men and women, sleeping or staggering. 'Twenty of them,' said Rhame proudly, 'and everyone guaranteed to have one point five per cent of alcohol in the blood or better. We'll keep them that way until we decide what to do next.'

'Only twenty?' demanded Cornut, suddenly alarmed. 'What about the others?' Rhame smiled like a shark. 'I see,' said Cornut, visioning that queer contradiction, a dead immortal. . . . Better, he told himself, than a dead planet.

He did not linger. He had to see Locille. Rhame had already phoned the campus and reported that she was well but still asleep; but Cornut needed first-hand assurance.

A police popper took him to the campus in a pelting rainstorm and he ran through the wet grass, looking around. The grass was stained and littered; the windows of the Med Centre showed where the mob had nearly smashed its way in. He hurried past, past the aborigines' camp, now deserted, past the Administration Building; past the memory of Master Carl and the Clinic where Egerd had died. The rain clouds stank of fumes from fires in the city; across the river there still lay thousands of unburied dead.

But the clouds were thin, and radiance began to shine through.

In his room, Locille stirred and woke. She was quite calm, and she smiled.

'I knew you'd be back,' she said. He took her in his arms, but even in that moment he could not forget what Rhame had told him, what they had already learned from the drunken, babbling immortals. The number of incipient telepaths was great indeed, as he had begun to suspect; but they were not 'abortions' of immortals, not at all.

They were the real thing. The mutation that had produced a St Cyr had produced many, many millions; it was not short-lived humans they had killed or driven to death, it was young immortals. The gene was a 'dominant, and now that it had shown so often it would soon fill the race. What the immortals had done was not to preserve themselves at the expense of a race that should have become extinct. They had only protected their own power against the Cornuts, the Locilles, the others with whom they did not wish to share.

'I knew you'd be back,' she whispered again.

'I told you I would,' he said. 'I'll always be back . . .' and he wondered how to tell her what 'always' had suddenly come to mean for them.

More about Penguins

If you have enjoyed reading this book you may
wish to know that *Penguin Book News* appears
every month. It is an attractively illustrated
magazine containing a complete list of books
published by Penguins and still in print, together
with details of the month's new books. A specimen
copy will be sent free on request.

Penguin Book News is obtainable from most
bookshops; but you may prefer to become a
regular subscriber at 3s. for twelve issues. Just
write to Dept EP, Penguin Books Ltd,
Harmondsworth, Middlesex, enclosing a cheque
or postal order, and you will be put on the
mailing list.

Some more science fiction published by Penguins
is described on the following pages.

Note: *Penguin Book News* is not available in the
U.S.A., Canada or Australia.

Who?

Algis Budrys

WHO WAS HE?... this man with a metal head and servo-mechanisms for jaws, eyes, ears...?

A Soviet plant? Martino – all that was left of him – brain-washed? Or simply Lucas Martino himself, the top allied scientist, reconstructed by Russian doctors from the unrecognizable dying fragments that had fallen into their hands when K-Eighty-eight went through the roof?

Had they got the secret of K-Eighty-eight, so oddly sited right on the Soviet border? Who was fooling who?

From the frantic efforts of Shawn Rogers, allied security chief, to prise the truth – the true truth – from a man in an iron mask, Algis Budrys, the brilliant new American SF writer, has built a story that, for gnawing tension, rivals John le Carré or Graham Greene.

'Constructs his book expertly, building up to the chilling irony of his solution' – Kingsley Amis in the *Observer*

Not for sale in the U.S.A. or Canada

The Black Cloud

Fred Hoyle

In 1964 a cloud of gas, of which there are a vast number in the universe, approaches the solar system on a course which is predicted to bring it between the Sun and the Earth, shutting off the Sun's rays and causing incalculable changes on our planet.

The effect of this impending catastrophe on the scientists and politicians is convincingly described by Fred Hoyle, the leading Cambridge astronomer: so convincingly, in fact, that the reader feels that these events may actually happen. This is science fiction at its very highest level.

'*The Black Cloud* is an exciting narrative, but, far more important, it offers a fascinating glimpse into the scientific power-dream' – Peter Green in the *Daily Telegraph*

'Mr Hoyle has written a really thrilling book . . . There is a largeness, generosity, and jollity about the whole spirit of the book that reminds one of the early Wells at his best' – *New Statesman*

'. . . The imagination is touched by this desperate effort by man to regain control of his environment by using his knowledge and his wits' – *The Times Literary Supplement*

'Mark: Alpha' – Maurice Richardson in the *Observer*

Not for sale in the U.S.A.

Lambda I and Other Stories

Edited by John Carnell

The eight top-line SF stories in this selection have been chosen by John Carnell from the best of a year's contributions to *New Worlds Science Fiction*. They include Colin Kapp's *Lambda I*, which reaches spine-chilling dimensions when a spacecraft, packed with a thousand passengers, loses its capacity to re-enter a normal environment. In *Quest*, by Lee Harding, an ordinary man looks for 'something real' in a world dominated by robots and megapolitan madness. The atomic submarine Taurus, in Philip E. High's *Routine Exercise*, returns to base with two dead men, minus its nuclear warheads, and a fantastic report of attack by an unknown craft.

'This is' (the editor writes) 'a cross-section of recently popular British science fiction which has been well-liked by many thousands of readers in different countries of the world.'

Not for sale in the U.S.A. or Canada

Connoisseur's Science Fiction

Edited by Tom Boardman

There is every sign that before long science fiction will be edging crime off the pavement. In this field few names are better known than that of Tom Boardman. He was the first reviewer in Britain to run a regular column on SF, is literary adviser to three publishers, and helped to found *S.F. Horizons*.

In this new anthology he has picked out ten of the SF stories that have given him most pleasure. To the general reader the names of the contributors that will probably stand out are Isaac Asimov, Frederik Pohl, Eric Frank Russell, Theodore Sturgeon, and Kurt Vonnegut. But if Tom Boardman's collection proves anything, it shows that there is a mounting number of writers producing stories which can be read and read again, in a field which commands a mounting number of readers every year.

Gunner Cade

Cyril Judd

TRAINED NOT TO THINK BEFORE KILLING
Cade was a mindless tool, one of a sworn brother-
hood of celibate armsmen, the Emperor's most
obedient servant.
But circumstances made Cade an outlaw, and
out of the peril of thought a man finds liberty
and love on this powerful fantasy of the future,
co-authored by the inimitable C. M. Kornbluth.

Not for sale in the U.S.A. or Canada

Mandrake

Susan Cooper

There were no stickers saying
'MANDRAKE MUST GO'
Instead, people's eyes clouded with awed
obedience at the mention of the all-powerful
Minister of Planning's name.
But why were people afraid?
Where had everyone gone?
What force was dragging Britain, city by city,
towards a horrible, unnatural end?
Was it
MANDRAKE?

Not for sale in the U.S.A.

J. G. Ballard

The Terminal Beach

THE CRYSTAL WORLD OF
J. G. BALLARD

where the white light of reason bends and
breaks into every shade of fear . . .
Twelve chill splinters of unreality

The Drowned World

'Ballard is one of the brightest new stars in
post-war fiction. This tale of strange and terrible
adventure in a world of steaming jungles has an
oppressive power reminiscent of Conrad' –
Kingsley Amis

The Four-Dimensional Nightmare

Man abandoned in a dry, decaying world of
automation.
Earth brushed by the tentacles of civilizations
from outer space. . . .
Time, music, poetry, beasts, and flowers
blossoming into new and garish forms.

Not for sale in the U.S.A.

Frederick Pohl

collaborates here with C. M. Kornbluth in
The Space Merchants

Time: a hundred years hence. Place: Madison
Avenue, New York. An overcrowded world is
dominated by giant advertising agencies which
do not stop short of armed warfare in their
struggles with one another. The President has
become a puppet, and the rest of the world has
been reduced to the status of drug-and-ad-
conditioned helots.

'Has many claims to being the best science
fiction novel so far' – Kingsley Amis in
New Maps of Hell

Not for sale in the U.S.A. or Canada